Shawn Amos
Illustrated by Robert Paul Jr.

Ⓛ Ⓑ
LITTLE, BROWN AND COMPANY
New York Boston

Little, Brown and Company
Hachette Book Group
1290 Avenue of the Americas, New York, NY 10104
Visit us at LBYR.com

First Edition: May 2022

Little, Brown and Company is a division of Hachette Book Group, Inc. The
Little, Brown name and logo are trademarks of Hachette Book Group, Inc.

The publisher is not responsible for websites (or their content) that are not
owned by the publisher.

"Mannish Boy"
Words and Music by Melvin London, Ellas McDaniel,
and McKinley Morganfield
© 1955 Arc Music Corp (BMI) / LONMEL Publishing Inc (BMI) [both
administered by BMG Rights Management (US) LLC]
Published by Watertoons Music.
Used by Permission. All Rights Reserved.

"(We've Got to) Come Together"
Written by Shawn Amos
Lyrics courtesy of Put Together Music (BMI)

Library of Congress Cataloging-in-Publication Data

Names: Amos, Shawn, author. Title: Cookies and milk / Shawn Amos.
Description: First edition. | New York : Little, Brown and Company, 2022. |
Based on the author's childhood. | Audience: Ages 8-12. | Summary:
Eleven-year-old Ellis discovers family secrets, makes new friends, and
adjusts to his parents' recent divorce during a hijinks-filled summer
helping his father open the world's first chocolate chip cookie store in
1976 Hollywood.
Identifiers: LCCN 2021032576 | ISBN 9780759556775 (hardcover) |
ISBN 9780759556768 (ebook)
Subjects: CYAC: Fathers and sons—Fiction. | Divorce—Fiction. |
Chocolate chip cookies—Fiction. | Entrepreneurship—Fiction. |
African Americans—Fiction. | LCGFT: Novels.
Classification: LCC PZ7.1.A499 Co 2022 | DDC [Fic]—dc23
LC record available at https://lccn.loc.gov/2021032576

ISBNs: 978-0-7595-5677-5 (hardcover),
978-0-7595-5676-8 (ebook)

Printed in the United States of America

LSC-C

Printing 1, 2022

This book is for my son and my father. I stand between you both as the three of us nurse our wounds across generations. This story is the bridge I have built for us. For you, my only son, I hope it also provides a light for your way forward.

This book is also dedicated to the young boys of all colors dreaming of the men they hope to become. Keep your eyes and your hearts open. There are clues all around you.

The Final Countdown

Sometimes you gotta take a chance.

This is it. My last moment to go out on top. Summer is one minute away. All eyes are on me. I slowly rip a small piece of paper from the corner of my notebook. I slip it into my mouth and start chewing. Next, I pull out the plastic straw I saved from lunch.

"Do it, Ellis," Alex whispers from his seat behind me.

Our math teacher, Mrs. Cook, is wiping the board, but she could turn around at any second. Her twisted gray hair is pulled on top of her head like a bird's nest sitting on a storm cloud. I quickly put the straw in my mouth. Using my tongue, I push the paper wad into the end of the straw. Showtime. The skinny red second hand on the clock moves up.

"Ten, nine, eight..." The class starts the countdown.

"Seven, six, five..." I aim at the center of Mrs. Cook's bird's nest.

"Four, three, two..." I blow as hard as I can.

"ONE!"

The spit wad flies through the air, rolling and tumbling. It's a perfect arc. Bullseye! It lands squarely on the back of Mrs. Cook's head—a lonely spit wad trapped in a tangled gray mess of hair. She doesn't suspect a thing. The bell rings and the class cheers.

"El-lis! El-lis! El-lis!" they chant.

My work here is done. That's it. Fifth grade is over. Years from now, students will still be talking about this moment. They might even rename the classroom after me: "The Ellis Bailey Johnson 1976 Memorial Spit Wad Classroom."

Everyone runs for the door, high-fiving me on the way out. Some of my friends whisper so Mrs. Cook doesn't hear.

"That was awesome, Ellis. Best one yet," Alex congratulates me. We immediately give each other our secret handshake—one palm slap, two fist bumps, then hook pinky fingers.

As I lift one foot over the classroom doorway for the last time, I feel a familiar tug on my backpack. Alex gives me a cringe look before slipping out of class. I turn around to see Mrs. Cook's stink eye looking down on me.

"Young man, I want to remind you that Hollywood Middle School will be receiving a long list of your..." She clears her throat. "... *extracurricular activities.*"

"Yes, Mrs. Cook." I'm careful to avoid her

glare and not inhale too deeply. Mrs. Cook's breath stinks almost as much as her eye.

"They will not be as tolerant as we have been here at Curtis Elementary School."

"Yes, Mrs. Cook." Her breath is choking me. I'm trying so hard to keep a straight face.

"It's a shame that such a smart boy wants to waste his time being a class clown." Mrs. Cook is always calling me a class clown. Can I help it if I think of funny stuff to do? "Enjoy your summer, young man." She releases my backpack. I watch Mrs. Cook return to the board with my spit wad in her hair. Then I get out of that classroom fast. Free at last.

Outside in the carpool line, summer vacation talk goes into overdrive as Alex hops in his dad's car.

"See you tonight at dinner, Ellis," Alex says as he closes the car door. They drive away, leaving me alone with Amanda Freeman. I am *so* glad Amanda is going to a different middle school next year. She's the worst. Always showing off. Amanda starts bragging about her trip to Hawaii before I can escape.

"So, my parents are letting me have my own hotel room. Now that I'm in middle school, they say I deserve to be treated like an adult." Amanda twists her hair as she brags a mile a minute. "Did you know Hawaii is called 'the Aloha State' and that the word *aloha* means 'love,' 'hello,' *and* 'good-bye'? I wrote my geography report on Hawaii. I got an A. What grade did you get?"

"I dunno, Amanda." I failed that report. I hate geography.

"Where are *you* going this summer, Ellis?"

Amanda actually asked me a question instead of talking more about herself? I'm so shocked that I start blabbing nonstop. "Nowhere. My parents just got divorced so my mom's gone for the summer. She's staying with her best friend in upstate New York. She says she needs to put herself first for a change. Well, first she said something I couldn't follow about being in a plane and putting on her oxygen mask first. Anyway, she's gone and it sucks. She's never left for more than a weekend. So I'm staying with my dad. That sucks even more."

Amanda looks at me and twists her hair. A piece of today's cafeteria lunch is wedged under her braces. Her eyes turn sad. Why did I say all that? I've only told Alex so far, and everyone knows that Amanda can't keep a secret.

"Oh, Ellis, I'm so sorry. Don't worry. I'm sure it'll be fine," Amanda says. She seems like she actually cares. For a split second, I think maybe it's okay that I told her. Then she keeps talking. "You know, I think it's really cute how you always make everyone laugh and how you play your harmonica all the time. And your hair is so funny and lumpy! All scrunchy-like. You remind me of my little brother. He's short and skinny like you."

Did I say how glad I am that Amanda is going to a different middle school next year?

"My dad's here. Look at his new car. Isn't it cool? Gotta go, Ellis. Aloha!" Amanda gives me a pat on my head then runs off.

Your hair is so funny and scrunchy. And a pat on my head? What is wrong with her? Please, *please* do not let me be the only Black kid in middle school next year. And please let me grow.

As the last of us wait for our rides, I pull my harmonica from my pocket and blow a few farewell notes. The harmonica is the best company you can keep. Blow into one of its ten holes and you get a note. Suck in the same hole and you get a totally different note. You can  suck in and blow in all sorts of combinations. Suck or blow a bunch of holes at the same time and it sounds like a huge wall of notes. The harmonica is like an orchestra in your pocket.

Amanda drives away in her dad's new silver sports car, revealing my dad's brown Rambler next in the carpool line. My dad's Rambler is the total opposite of a sports car. It's old. *Really* old. Dad says it's got a "vibe." I'd rather have the vibe of a school bus taking me home. It'd be less embarrassing.

Dad leans over and opens the car door from the inside. The outside handle doesn't work anymore. "What's up, Little Man?" he says.

"Don't call me that," I say for the millionth time.

Dad's Rambler is beat-up, but it sure smells good—like brown sugar and cocoa. I toss my backpack on the floor, stuff my harmonica in my pocket, then slide across the big bench seat. The front dashboard is covered in pins, buttons, and a few decals. The KEEP ON TRUCKIN' button used to be on my backpack. My DYN-O-MITE! button is also there. It's from my favorite TV show, *Good Times*. A guy named J.J. always says "Dyn-o-mite!" when he's excited. All of the other buttons are Dad's. There's a big yellow one with a happy face. It stares at me while we're driving. Some of the other buttons have phrases like SUPPORT YOUR LOCAL FEMINIST. The strangest one has a picture of a smiling peanut with the words CARTER FOR PRESIDENT. A peanut for president?

Dad slides that familiar wrinkled paper bag across the bench seat toward me. The sugary smell has fully invaded my nose. It's hard to believe a smell can make you forget your troubles, but sometimes it's true. Right now, the smell in that bag is quickly making me forget about my summer.

My Dad, the Cookie Man

I made a fresh batch," Dad says as he hands me the bag. It's warm in my hands. I open it and pull out one of Dad's chocolate chip cookies. He's been making them for as long as I can remember. He says it relaxes him and helps him think.

And his cookies taste good. I mean really, REALLY good. They're like bite-sized crunchy golden cookie nuggets. Each one is packed with gooey chocolate chips and sweet pecans.

I could eat his cookies and nothing else.

Before the divorce, we baked cookies all the time. I'm trying to remember the last time we made them, but I can't. Since the divorce, everything is screwed up.

"Well?" Dad asks. He always wants my opinion. It's kinda pitiful.

"Pretty good," I say.

"What's that?" he says as he pokes me in the rib. "You're mumbling, Little Man. I can't hear you."

"They taste pretty good." I make sure to pronounce every word clearly. Both of my parents tell me that I mumble. All I know is that sometimes it's hard for me to speak when I get nervous or mad.

Dad steals a cookie from my bag. He pops it in his mouth. "Not *bad*?!" he says while crunching the cookie. "Man, these are *fantastic*."

"Don't talk with cookies in your mouth. It's rude," I scold him. After all, that's what he and Mom are always telling me.

"Some things, Ellis, cannot wait to be said." He pulls out another one of MY cookies. Dad stretches his right arm up and out in front of him toward the front windshield. It's like his arm is a telescope and at the end is a small, crunchy chocolate chip asteroid suspended against the clear blue California sky.

"Look at you," Dad says admiringly to the cookie. Dad doesn't just eat cookies. He *talks* to them like they're pets or friends. My dad is like that Willy Wonka chocolate factory guy. I don't remember everything about the book, but I do know that if Willy Wonka was tall, skinny, Black, and had a salt-and-pepper beard, he would be my dad. I really think Dad believes that chocolate chip cookies have some kind of magical power.

Dad continues talking to the cookie in his hand. "You are perfect. Just the right amount of chips. And look at that lightly toasted pecan poking through. YOU are a good cookie!" Then he retracts his telescope arm and pops the cookie in his mouth.

"Isn't it kind of weird to eat something you love so much?" I ask.

"No, no," Dad says. "Chocolate chip cookies are *meant* to be eaten. It's their life's purpose to bring joy."

"That doesn't make any sense. What if I was born just to be eaten?"

"Then you'd be a chocolate chip cookie."

Dad steers his Rambler through the traffic on Sunset Boulevard. Some people call it "the Sunset

Strip." It's full of famous nightclubs and shops. I don't come down here all that often. Sunset Boulevard is full of strange characters. Mom always says, "Sunset Strip is no place for little boys."

I see our street corner approaching. Usually, Dad would turn left off Sunset and drop me off at Mom's house. Not today. Dad drives farther east into Sunset Boulevard. I've never been this far down Sunset. We approach Ralphs supermarket. People in the neighborhood call it "Rock and Roll Ralphs" because lots of famous singers and bands go there late at night. Rock and Roll Ralphs is huge. It's a whole other world inside. The grocery store takes up the entire block, and it never closes. Out front there's always a weird mix of little kids on kiddie rides, teenagers smoking, and old men feeding pigeons.

A few blocks from the Rock and Roll Ralphs, Dad stops the car at the corner of Sunset and Formosa. We're parked in front of a small empty building. It's funny looking, shaped like a triangle and with a door at the bottom, a window in each corner, and a chimney sticking out of the pointy top.

It's seriously run-down. The stucco white paint is peeling above the front glass doors. A family of pigeons have pooped all over the roof.

This is not the glamorous part of Sunset. This block is on the edge of Hollywood. It feels a world away from our house a few miles behind us. This block looks creepy. And sad. Most of the stores are abandoned. Trash is blowing down the sidewalk. This empty store looks like an abandoned house in the middle of a bad fairy tale. Weeds surround it. A paper sign saying RENTED is taped over another paper sign that says FOR RENT.

I roll down the car window. It gets stuck halfway like it always does. I sit up on my knees so I can speak over the glass. "Dad, what is this?"

"You're mumbling, Little Man," Dad says with his back to me. He's looking at the top of the pointy roof.

"Stop calling me Little Man! I'm eleven years old," I yell in my head.

Dad whips around. "What did you say to me?"

Oops. I yelled that out loud.

"You don't listen. Just like Mom says." I definitely said *that* out loud.

"Get out of the car, Ellis," my dad orders.

I open the car door and get out. Dad and I face each other like in one of those cowboy movies. He leans over me. He runs his hand across his beard then speaks in his most serious voice. "Now, *you* listen to *me*, Little Man. I am still your father, divorce or no divorce. You want to know what this is? This A-frame is our home for the summer."

"Home?" I squeeze my eyes shut to keep my tears in. There's no way I want Dad to see me cry.

"Yep. Our new home for our new *cookies*. Six weeks from now we're gonna open the world's first chocolate chip cookie store." Dad looks up at the building. He's grinning ear to ear. My eyes go dry. Now I'm just confused.

"The world's *what*?" A store that only sells *cookies*? *Chocolate chip* cookies? How is that even a thing? How can anyone make money just selling chocolate chip cookies? No one has EVER opened a store selling just chocolate chip cookies. That's totally crazy.

Dad looks up at the front of the building. He's starry-eyed like he's sitting in the first row of a movie theater. "A cookie store," he repeats. "And you and I are gonna build it together."

"Great," I say sarcastically while I roll my eyes. "Happy birthday to me."

Dad opens the front door. "What's that about your birthday? It's only June. Now get inside. We've got work to do."

I'm stuck in place. This cannot be my summer.

"Did you hear me?" Dad thumps the back of my head.

"Uh-huh," I mumble as I walk inside.

"Ellis, you dropped something getting out of the car." Dad hands me my harmonica. "You don't wanna lose this. We're going to need some music."

I'm gonna need more than music to get through this nightmare. I wish Mom would come home. What the heck are Dad and I going to talk about for six weeks? Alone. In an abandoned store on Sunset Boulevard. This was supposed to be my epic twelfth-birthday summer. I can't believe this is my life.

Another Bad Idea

I immediately hold my nose as I enter. "It smells like old cigarettes in here."

"How do *you* know what old cigarettes smell like?" Dad asks.

"I know from looking at this carpet." The sea of neon orange shag carpet is littered with cigarette butts. It looks like an old, faded itchy sweater exploded all over the floor. It also *stinks*. Actually, the more I get a whiff of it, this carpet looks and smells like a wet, itchy sweater that a shaggy dog wore in the rain. A dog that smokes but never bathes. And whose sweater exploded all over this floor. Okay, maybe that was too much. But you get the point.

"Dad, this place is gross. You can't sell cookies here," I say, trying to plug my nose and speak at the same time. "And who sells nothing but chocolate chip cookies anyway? Ice cream store? I get it. Doughnuts? Yes. But *cookies*? And just one kind of cookie?"

Now I'm remembering all of Dad's old dumb ideas. There was Stone Fruit Jewels, Dad's idea to sell handmade jewelry made of polished cherry, peach, and apricot pits. Then there was Dapper Dogs. Dad was going to sell designer footwear for... you guessed it...dogs. One time, he was going to open a store called American Dashiki. A *dashiki* is a super colorful shirt that people wear in West Africa. I had a hard time remembering the word when I first heard it, so I made a rhyme to help me: My *dashiki* looks *freaky*. American Dashiki was one of Dad's dumbest ideas. Mom told him there were three problems with it:

1. We live in Hollywood, California, *not* West Africa.
2. We are basically the only Black people in Hollywood, California.
3. White people don't wear dashikis.

"Everybody loves chocolate chip cookies, Ellis. Everybody!" Dad says. "This place will make us—"

THWACK!

Dad and I jump. Grandma Ruby is at the front door, whacking the glass with her cane.

"Junior!" she yells. Grandma's cane isn't just to help her walk on her bad knees. Her cane is a weapon. I've seen her swing that cane at pigeons, paperboys, and park benches. When something upsets Grandma, she swings first and asks questions later. Luckily, her aim is really bad. So is her vision. She shouldn't be driving, but I see her white Cadillac parked behind Dad's Rambler.

Dad runs to open the door. Grandma enters, and swats her cane at Dad like he's a mosquito. "What you doin' bringing that boy here?" she demands. Grandma is tough but also protective. I know she loves me. But, man, she scares me.

"Mama, I'm a forty-four-year-old man. Stop calling me Junior. And put that cane down before you hurt somebody." Dad laughs as he closes and locks the front door behind her. It *is* kind of funny seeing Grandma in her hairnet, holding her cane in one hand, her beige leather purse hanging from her other forearm, and her baggy pantyhose bunched up around her ankles like saggy skin. I would never let her see me laugh, though. I don't want that cane anywhere near me.

"This boy ain't got no business in all this mess! Sunset Boulevard ain't no place for a little boy," she scolds Dad while pulling me close. "You think you're gonna make *cookies* in here?" *THWACK!* Grandma's cane smashes a cigarette butt and sends a cockroach flying as if from a circus cannon. "You better call an *exterminator* in here."

"Ellis and I have this all under control, Mama. Don't we, Little Man?"

"Um-hm," I mumble.

"Stay here, Mama," Dad says. "I'm going back in the kitchen to make sure we have water and power running."

Dad disappears into the back while Grandma scans her eyes around the inside of the empty store. I try and wriggle away, but she quickly pulls me back into her.

"Boy, come here," she orders.

I hate those three words. *Boy. Come. Here.* Those words are *not* to be trusted. Let me tell you a short story so you know why.

One time—before Grandma moved to California—we visited her in Tallahassee, Florida. I knocked over her favorite candle while I was running in the house. The candle wasn't lit or anything. It didn't even break. I picked it up superfast, put it back on her coffee table, and quickly apologized. End of story, right?

Wrong.

"Boy, come here."

Uh-oh. Those words.

"You go out back. Get me a switch," she ordered me.

In case you don't know, a *switch* is a really thin tree branch. It's so thin that it makes a whistling sound when you wave it in the air. When Grandma Ruby asks for a switch, you know you're in trouble. It's worse than a belt. You can guess how the story ends. My butt still hurts thinking about it.

But I haven't done anything wrong *today*. Not yet. Plus, there is nowhere to get a switch on Sunset Boulevard. I stay close to Grandma, guessing I'm safe but keeping an eye on her cane just in case.

"Boy, I'm gonna tell you something your daddy won't never say." Grandma looks down at me, leaning heavily on her cane.

"I can hear you, Mama!" Dad yells from the back.

"Good!" she yells back. "It means your ears are working better than that brain of yours." Grandma continues loud enough for Dad to hear. "Your daddy don't know one thing about openin' up no cookie store. Just like he didn't know nothing about selling no dashikis or opening up a disco car wash."

Dad defends himself from the back. "The disco car wash would have worked. I just needed to figure out how to waterproof the speakers. That's not easy."

"Uh-hmm." Grandma is not impressed. She then lowers her voice like she has a secret. She pulls me close and whispers in my ear, "That daddy of yours has lots of dumb ideas. But I know he loves you. More than you know. So you gonna need to—"

THWACK!

Did Grandma just whack me with her cane? I check my body. I check her cane. My body is intact. Her cane hasn't moved.

"Junior!" Grandma yells. "You alright back there?"

Slippin' in the Darkness

It's pitch-black inside the kitchen with only a tiny sliver of light escaping from the front of the store.

"Dad? Are you okay?" I ask into the darkness.

Suddenly, Dad's face appears. He looks like one of those faces in horror movies or slumber party ghost stories. One hand holds a flashlight. The other is grabbing his knee. Next to him, it looks like a jet engine has crashed from the sky. The shiny metal glistens as it rocks from side to side, like the last wobbly moments of a spinning top. The metal against the concrete floor makes a hollow clanking sound.

Dad winces as he explains, "The lights shut off! Strangest thing. I haven't even gotten a bill yet, so I know it wasn't the power company. I'm not going through that hassle again."

"That hassle" is the time our power got turned off at the house. Mom and I sat in the dark all night. Mom was so mad—and not only because Dad forgot to pay the bill. He also left the house as soon as the lights went out. He said he couldn't think in the dark, so he sat in his Rambler for hours. I watched the neighbors' TV through my bedroom window.

Dad manages to stand up on his hurt knee. Now I see what fell: a big metal bowl. He pushes it upright. "I smacked right into the mixing bowl in the dark." He shines the flashlight on a crack. "Uh-oh. Metal mixing bowls aren't supposed to break. How am I gonna get this fixed?"

"That's a mixing bowl? I could take a bath in there."

Dad kind of laughs, but I can tell he's stressed. "I guess you could, Little Man. We need something bigger than my ceramic mixing bowl. This one will make us two hundred pounds of cookie dough at a time."

"Two hundred pounds of cookie dough? Who could even bake that many cookies?"

"We're going to find out," Dad assures me. Then he recites a list: "Fine-tune our recipe, get our ingredients, fix this store, and find our customers. That's all that matters for the next six weeks. But first we're going to need to get these lights back on. Then we need to buy all of the bags of chocolate chips that we can carry."

Grandma yells from the front, "Buying chocolate chips ain't the only thing you need to do." Grandma follows Dad's flashlight into the kitchen. "Junior, shine that light here, in my pocketbook," she orders him. "And take my cane. Looks like you could use it."

Grandma calls her purse a "pocketbook." It's something old ladies do. It rocks back and forth on her outstretched forearm like a playground swing. I can briefly see what's inside before the purse swings away from the light. Grandma is getting frustrated. "Hold that light still, Junior. You're giving me a headache."

"Hold your *purse* still, Mama," Dad replies.

"You get your own cane if you're going to talk

back to me!" Grandma scolds him before taking back her walking stick. Then she yells into the darkness, "NOT TODAY, SATAN! I ain't got no time for this mess! I need these lights back on!"

And just like that, the lights flicker back on.

Now listen...I know for *sure* that Grandma does *not* have any superpowers. But I can say this: When she gets annoyed (and that is almost *all* the time), she will yell, "NOT TODAY, SATAN!" And when she does, things change. I don't understand it. I don't ask any questions. I just accept it as a fact.

Grandma holds her purse motionless and says to me, "Boy, get me my pen and pad." I reach inside and grab her small writing pad and pen. Grandma places them on the counter. The purse stays on her forearm. Grandma's purse *always* stays on her forearm.

Grandma rips off two pieces of paper. She starts writing in all capital letters. Each letter is shaky— like it might fall onto the letter next to it. She hands one piece of paper to Dad and the other to me. Mine has a strange word.

FITTT

I look at Dad's. Another strange word.

LITTT

"Here. You two come on back when you've figured this out. I'm going outside to pull up those weeds before they drive me crazy." Grandma heads to the front of the store, leaving me and Dad to wonder.

"Fit? Lit?" I read the "words" out loud, trying to make sense of them. "What the heck do these mean? And why did she spell them wrong?"

"Your grandma loves her acronyms," Dad says, shaking his head at the paper. "When I was your age, maybe a little younger, she would say things like, 'You better *git*.' G.I.T., which means 'Get. It. Together.' But I've never seen *these* acronyms."

I say each letter of the acronyms out loud.

F.I.T.T.T.

L.I.T.T.T.

It still doesn't make any sense. But one thing I *do* know about Grandma: Don't expect her to make sense. Dad flips the light switch on and off. He's still wondering why the power went out.

"This power better not be an issue," Dad says. "I can't afford any setbacks."

"Not today, Satan," I tell him.

"That's right, Little Man." Dad rubs the top of my head like I'm a good luck statue. The only thing worse than being called "Little Man" is having your head rubbed after being called "Little Man." Ugh. Dad will never get it.

"C'mon," Dad says, sticking his LITTT note in his pocket. "Grandma's secret language can wait. We need to get down to the Rock and Roll Ralphs and get our chocolate chips."

"Why do I have to go?" I ask before sticking my FITTT note in my pocket.

"Because this is *our* store," Dad says. "And four hands are better than two."

I groan. This is *not* my store. And Grandma's right—he doesn't know *anything* about opening a chocolate chip cookie store. He doesn't even have any chocolate chips. And most importantly, I'm a kid. Like Grandma said, I ain't got no business in all this mess. A kid should be outside for the summer, not trapped inside an abandoned store. Man, I hope every single bag of chocolate chips is sold out at the Rock and Roll Ralphs. No chocolate chips, no chocolate chip cookie store.

The Chocolate Chips Come Crashing Down

Look at them, Ellis. What a beautiful sight."

Well, so much for every bag of chocolate chips being sold. Dad and I are standing in aisle ten of the Rock and Roll Ralphs. The baking aisle. Dad looks up at a wall of chocolate chip bags stacked above our heads. It's definitely enough to make two hundred pounds of dough.

Each bag is yellow with a clear section in the middle where you can see the chocolate chips peeking through. They look like a bunch of chocolate-chip-filled beanbags stacked on top of one another.

Dad stares at them like he's watching a TV set. He looks a little freaky, like he's in a daydream.

"You know what this reminds me of?" Dad asks.

"Cookies?" I reply.

"That's a good guess, but no. Looking at all of these chocolate chips reminds me of my aunt Della."

"Aunt Della?" I ask. I lean forward on our empty shopping cart. I've heard Aunt Della's name a couple of times. Dad doesn't like talking about the past, or his family, but he makes an exception for Aunt Della. I never met her, though. She died long before I was born.

"Aunt Della is the first person who ever baked chocolate chip cookies for me." Dad starts to describe Aunt Della's cookies—still in his daydream.

"It was the winter of 1945. I was almost eleven years old. Mama and Daddy just got divorced. Daddy was long gone, and Mama sent me to live with Aunt Della in New York. Mama said she would meet me there as soon as she could. It was my very first train ride. She packed me a tomato sandwich in my shoeshine kit. I was making money shining shoes in Florida. I thought I could earn a dollar or two polishing shoes for people on the train. I got to New York almost an entire day later."

It's like Dad's transported himself back to 1945. I never knew Dad's parents divorced, too.

"Aunt Della greeted me as soon as I walked off the train. She had so much joy bursting out of her. She gave me the biggest hug I've ever had in my life. Aunt Della loved to give hugs. Man, I thought I was gonna suffocate in her wool overcoat."

"Dad, are we gonna get the chocolate chips?" I ask. He doesn't hear me. He's still daydreaming. I roll back and forth on the shopping cart.

"It was almost dark outside when we got to her apartment. I couldn't believe my eyes when she opened the door. Aunt Della had a sofa bed pulled out in the living room just for me. Back in Florida, I slept on a cot in the same room as Mama and Daddy.

"She went straight into the kitchen. I expected her to start cooking collard greens or biscuits or catfish. That's what Mama would be making around this time. Instead, Aunt Della was measuring cups of sugar and flour. Then she opened a bag of chocolate chips. I had never seen *anyone* make cookies."

Dad turns around to look at me. "When I tasted that cookie, Little Man, it tasted like home." Dad pauses for a moment before finishing. "I wish you could've met her. Aunt Della was somethin' else."

Dad snaps out of his daze. "Alright, I'm gonna get a few other things, Little Man. You put about..." Dad interrupts himself to count the cash in his pocket. "...twenty bags in the cart. That's all we can afford today. It'll get us started, though. We've gotta learn how to make a lot of cookies."

Dad rounds the corner out of view. I look up at the wall of chocolate chips. I try to grab the top bag of the stack, but it's just out of reach. This has happened before. I've gotten used to climbing onto the kitchen counter at home to grab a bowl or a glass from the cabinet. *Please* let me grow this summer.

Climbing a grocery store shelf can't be much different than climbing up a kitchen counter. I pull my harmonica from my pocket and blow six notes from low to high like a battle charge. *Dah-dah-dah-dah-dah-DAH*. Then I slide my left foot in between two bags of flour on the second shelf. Using my right hand, I pull myself up, careful to avoid knocking over the small cartons of baking soda in front of my fingertips. If I can climb up one more shelf, I should be able to grab the bags and toss them into the cart.

I stretch my left arm up as far as possible. Pinching the corner of a bag between my thumb and index finger, I slowly wiggle it off the top of the stack. I can feel the weight of the bag as it enters into the palm of my hand. I need to focus.

"CLEANUP ON AISLE SIX, DAIRY. CLEANUP ON AISLE SIX."

The booming voice through the speaker above my head completely shocks me. I lose my balance. My fingers are losing their grip. I'm like a dog paddling in the water as I try to hold on to anything that will keep me standing upright on the shelf. And I do! I grab a bag of chocolate chips. Uh-oh. Bad idea. The bag slowly slides off the shelf. The other bags quickly follow in one big chocolate chip avalanche. I fall back onto the ground. Bag after bag of chocolate chips land on top of me. Some break wide

open. As I am buried alive in chocolate chips, I hear an urgent voice boom through the store speaker above my head.

"CLEANUP ON AISLE TEN, BAKING. CLEAN-UP ON AISLE TEN."

Man, I hate being short. *Please* let me grow this summer.

Dad and I stand in the checkout line. My shirt is covered in chocolate chip dust. I keep my head down. This is not my proudest moment. The cashier eyes my chocolate-stained shirt then asks, "Did you find everything you need?"

"We most certainly did," my dad answers. "But sadly, much of it slipped away."

Dad pulls some money out of his pocket. "So… we will pay you for these thirteen broken bags of chocolate chips on aisle ten and these seven bags here."

"Dad, I'm sorry," I mumble. "I wasted your money and all of those chocolate chips."

Dad hands the cashier his cash then looks at

me. "Oh, don't worry, you're going to pay me back." That doesn't sound good.

"I hate being short. I hate it so much." I meant to say that to myself, but I ended up saying it out loud. Dad doesn't hear me, as usual.

But he does smile as he gets his change from the cashier. "Come on down the street if you're in the mood for some chocolate chip cookies. We're gonna be selling them real soon."

The cashier giggles at Dad. I can see she tried to stop herself, but she couldn't. "A store selling chocolate chip cookies?" she says in amazement. "Well, that is something I have to see." She looks at me and asks, "Will you be helping?"

"Yes, he will." Dad steps in before I have a chance to tell her *No, I will* not *be helping*.

"That's sweet. A father and son cookie store. I look forward to tasting them."

"*We* look forward to it," Dad responds. We walk away, but Dad quickly turns back. "Oh, and by the way." He pauses. "Before we open our store, we're going to need more chocolate chips. Can you tell me when you expect your next delivery?"

The cashier gives Dad the same look Mom sometimes gives me. It's the look that says, "You have no idea what you're doing, do you?" Finally, she answers, "Check back next week. We might have more by then. You could also check Thrifty Supermarket on Fairfax Avenue."

Dad quickly responds, "Not a chance. We'll wait. This is our supermarket. Us neighborhood businesses need to support each other."

A chocolate chip cookie store without any chocolate chips. This whole thing is a mess. We have no idea what we are doing. All I can hear is Grandma's voice saying "G.I.T." Six weeks doesn't seem like a lot of time to open a store. Man, I hope nothing else goes wrong. I hope *I* don't make anything else go wrong.

The Fire-Breathing Oven

School is back in session." Dad is mixing cookie dough in his favorite, chipped ceramic mixing bowl. The one he uses at home. He stares into it like he might reach his hand inside and pull out a rabbit. I can't get Grandma's acronyms out of my head: FITTT, LITTT.

Without looking up, Dad repeats his list again: "Fine-tune our recipe, get our ingredients, fix this store, and find our customers." Then he continues. "There's a lot of math involved in making cookies,

Little Man. First thing we need to do is fine-tune our recipe so we can make a MUCH bigger batch of cookies."

Grandma enters through the kitchen back door. She dumps an armful of weeds into the garbage can. "Ain't nobody in this family know nothin' about math," she snorts.

"Ellis does, Mama," Dad replies. "He could be the first Johnson to go to college. *If* he can stop fooling around in school." Dad looks up from his bowl. He continues explaining cookie dough math to me. "We can only make a few dozen cookies in this little bowl. We'll easily need many times that amount when the store opens. So, *your* job is to figure out how we make the cookie recipe bigger."

"But, Dad, it's summer," I protest.

"And you owe me for thirteen broken bags of chocolate chips. Stop whining. We've got a problem to solve. And you have the skills to do it."

"Fine," I mumble.

"Excellent. Now let's test bake this small batch." Dad turns to the big metal rectangular box behind him. It's as tall as Dad, perched on four slightly arched legs, with four thick handles on the front. Each one opens a giant metal door.

"Shouldn't an oven have a window so you can see inside?" I ask suspiciously.

"Not this one. You just need to keep track of time with this baby," Dad says. He pats the side of the oven proudly. He then turns a large red dial. I can hear the oven ignite—as if a rocket engine just launched. "We can bake almost eight hundred cookies in this thing. C'mon, Little Man, let's get these into the oven." He scoops a big sticky mound of sugary cookie dough on the baking sheet in front of me. Chocolate chips and pecans stick out like jagged rocks. I can't help but pull out a few chips and nuts. I savor them in my mouth. This is the first time Dad and I have made cookies in a while.

"I'll race you to the end of the baking sheet," Dad dares me. This is how we used to make cookies. A competition to see who can "drop" cookies the fastest. *Dropping* is when you place small pinches of cookie dough in neat rows across the baking sheet. It's not as easy as it sounds. If you place them too closely, they'll bleed into one another. You'll have one big cookie. Place them too far apart, and you'll waste space on the baking sheet. Dad taught me that you should drop about four dozen cookies on a baking sheet. That's eight rows of cookies. I guess he's right that there is a lot of math involved in baking. Of course, he never asks if I *like* doing these dumb races—which I don't.

"Ready, set, GO!" Dad starts the dropping race. I grab a handful of dough from the giant mound and start pinching off pieces. Each "drop" looks like an oversized doughy gumball on my baking sheet. I look at Dad's end of the baking sheet. He's already dropped three rows! What the heck? The dough is getting sticky in my hands. It's difficult to pinch off a drop. I start eating dough from my fingers to clean them.

"Ellis! You cannot lick your fingers then put them back in the dough," Dad lectures me. "Hands stay clean. Always."

"But I need to get the dough to stop sticking to them." I say, sucking my fingers. It's so creamy it almost melts in my mouth.

"Remember the trick?" Dad takes a bit of flour and sprinkles it across his small mound of dough. "A pinch of flour keeps it from sticking." Dad drops his last row of cookie dough on the baking sheet. His hands are totally clean. No cookie dough on

them. Ugh. He always wins. Shouldn't a dad let his kid win sometimes?

"Next time, Little Man. Now, you get these cookies baked. Set the timer for twelve minutes. I'm going to see how Grandma is doing pullin' up all those weeds. She loves her gardening. I'm gonna get her a little greenhouse in the back to keep her busy."

Dad walks out front while I stare at this beast of an oven in front of me. I can almost hear a dragon inside belching flames. I slowly walk toward it. My heart is beating so hard I can feel it in my throat. This does not seem right. Shouldn't you need a license to operate this? I reach for the thick chrome handle and slowly pull down the oven door. A wave of heat slaps my face and stings my eyes. I place Dad's baking sheet inside and slam the oven door shut before I melt.

When Dad and I made cookies at home, I would sit down in front of the oven with my harmonica. I'd blow while I watched the cookies turn golden brown through the glass. I can't do that here. This oven is a fortress. I can't even sit down comfortably on this hard concrete floor. What fun is baking cookies if you can't see what you're baking? This is boring. This place does *not* feel like a home.

I pull my harmonica from my pocket and raise it to my mouth. I hold it like a sandwich between my index fingers and thumbs. I blow my first note and...it tastes like cookie dough. Uh-oh, my hands are still covered in sticky batter. The first rule of harmonica: Keep your hands and mouth clean. Time to wash up so I can practice.

F.I.T.T.

The bathroom in this store is pretty gross—just like the rest of the place. I think about Dad's list: fine-tune our recipe, get our ingredients, fix this store, and find our customers. It's going to take *a lot* of work to fix this store. There's a dirty sink attached to a grimy wall. A rectangular metal shelf sits right above it. And above the shelf is a mirror almost entirely covered with stickers. The biggest one says GROOVY, written in squishy letters like a cloud. There's another sticker of a white bird holding a daisy in its beak. Some of the stickers had been peeled off so there's just a white-and-brown smear left behind.

Mom would kill me if I put stickers all over our bathroom mirror at home. She's already annoyed at how much time I spend in there. You see, here's something most people don't know about bathrooms—even bathrooms as gross as this one. They are great places to play harmonica. Mr. Gidnick taught us a word for it in music class: reverb. You know those cartoons when someone yells in a cave and their voice keeps echoing forever? That's reverb. Bathrooms have reverb. The sound bounces around everywhere. You should try it.

I clap my hands to test the reverb. This bathroom isn't nearly as good as the one at home. Still, my hand clap echoes a couple of times, so I know there's a bit of reverb. I wash the cookie dough from my hands, dry them on my jeans, and pull my harmonica from my pocket. Before I play, I make sure there's no bits of pecans in my mouth. You don't want a piece of food getting stuck in your harmonica like that lunch in Amanda Freeman's braces. Mouth is clean. Now I raise my harmonica to my lips and make a sound like an oncoming train. *Chug-a-chug-a-chug.* I close my eyes. Sometimes I like to imagine how I look before I actually *see* how I look. In my mind, I'm playing onstage. The crowd is shouting my name. I step in front of the band. My chugging sound turns into a rumbling harmonica solo. I'm bending notes low and high. My mouth speeds back and forth on my harmonica.

I can hear the reverb of the audience clapping. I can almost smell…

"SMOKE!!!"

A thick layer of gray smoke is crawling under the bathroom door. It soon covers my feet.

"Ellis!" I hear Dad yelling from the kitchen. My heart is back in my throat again. I quickly stick my harmonica in my pocket.

Outside the bathroom, Dad is fanning the smoke

with a baking sheet. Grandma swings the back door open and shut a few times, then disappears outside. The whole place smells like a burnt cookie campfire.

"I told you to watch the cookies. What happened?" Dad sounds more concerned than mad. He stares at the tray of burnt cookies. My heart is now pounding in my *head*, not my throat. I can barely answer him.

"I…I…I went to the bathroom. I was playing my harmonica," I confess.

"Playing your harmonica is *not* watching the cookies," Dad replies as the last of the smoke floats out of the back door. He holds out his hand. Now he's mad. "Give it to me."

"No, Dad, I'm sorry. You can't take my harmonica," I beg. Dad doesn't even care. He grabs the end of the harmonica and pulls it from my pocket.

"No more distractions. No more climbing on shelves. No more hiding out in the bathroom with this." Dad pokes my harmonica in my chest. "We've got six weeks to open this store. It's day ONE! We have a broken mixer, not enough chocolate chips, and a bunch of burnt cookies. I cannot have any more setbacks. Now you get outside, help your grandma, and think about how you're going to make this right. And no more messing around with this stupid harmonica. You won't get it back next time. I promise."

Dad tosses the harmonica to me. It falls to the concrete floor before I can catch it. I quickly scoop it up. One of the metal covers is scratched.

"The only stupid thing here is this store," I blurt out before I can take it back. But it's true. His cookies are more important than me. I stuff my harmonica back in my pocket and run out the back door.

Standing in the parking lot, I check the scratch on my harmonica. It's going to bug me every time I see it. I rub my finger on it and give it a blow. It's better than yelling. Then I hear those three words from around the corner.

"Boy, come here."

Uh-oh. Grandma is calling. I slowly walk to the edge of the parking lot. I look to my left. I see her sitting in a folding chair on the side of the A-frame store. She's pulling some stubborn weeds from the cracks of the sidewalk. Grandma wears her big floppy sun hat. Her cane is on the ground next to her. It's definitely within reach. I better be careful. She stares down into the weeds just like Dad was staring into the mixing bowl. Her bony hands yank a long, skinny twig from the ground. Without looking up she hands it to me.

"Take this switch, boy."

I gulp. Is she gonna give me a switch? In front of all of Hollywood, California? Grandma keeps pulling weeds. She's still not looking at me.

"Now throw it on that pile with them other ones," she says.

Whew, it's my lucky day. I toss the switch on a dirty pile of weeds, twigs, and leaves.

"Go on and play me something on that harmonica of yours."

Wow, Grandma wants me to play? I make my chugging sound. Grandma nods her approval. "It reminds me of being back in Tallahassee," she says. Then she adjusts her floppy sun hat. I know Grandma didn't call me over here just to hear my harmonica. She has something on her mind.

"Boy, show me that paper I gave you."

I pull her notepad paper from my pocket and hold it in front of her.

"You best remember to keep fit—F.I.T.T.T." Grandma spells it out, yanking another thick green weed from the ground on the final *T*.

I look at Grandma blankly. I best remember to keep fit? Does Grandma think I should exercise?

"You ain't got no clue, do you, boy?"

Isn't it obvious?

"I'm going to tell you this once," Grandma says in a rare display of mercy. "You need all the help you can get with that stubborn head of yours. Just like your daddy." She then reveals the answer like a secret kept hidden for years. "Family is tougher than time."

"Huh?" I respond.

"Don't back talk me, boy. I'll take that switch to your Black bottom right now." Grandma lays down her weed and continues. "We are family. It don't matter about no divorce. It don't matter about no arguments. It don't matter how much you're mad at your daddy. We are still family. Forever. Ain't nothing gonna change that. That oven, that mixer, these darn weeds—they all are gonna pass in time. But family remains. No matter how big or small. Family is tougher than time. F.I.T.T.T."

Grandma reaches over me. She grabs the switch from the pile of weeds and raises it up over her head. "Now, boy, you better run your Black butt back in that store before I get it with this switch. No more nonsense. Now, *git*!"

"Yes, ma'am," I say as politely as possible. I run back to the parking lot, and suddenly things look a lot better.

I think I see my ride out of this store.

Mr. Reedy to the Rescue

Alex!" I yell from across the parking lot. We immediately give each other our secret handshake—one palm slap, two fist bumps, then grab pinky fingers. "What are you doing here?" I ask.

"Your dad said you could spend the night after dinner," Alex replies. "He already talked to your mom about it."

Dad and Mom talked?

Alex continues. "Now we have more time to play albums on our turntable." Alex and I usually meet up after school to play records. Someday we're going to start a band together—even though Alex doesn't know how to play anything. It takes a true best friend to join your band even if he doesn't play an instrument.

Alex's dad gets out of the car. Mr. Reedy is way older than my dad. He's bald on the top of his head with a ring of white hair on the sides and back. He wears the kind of glasses that make you look smart. The kind you might take off your face with one hand then stick in your mouth while you try to solve a really complicated problem. He walks over and puts his shaky hand on my shoulder. He then asks in his familiar, slightly halting voice, "So this is the home of Sunset Cookies, huh?"

Dad's calling the store Sunset Cookies? Well, there's another thing he didn't bother to tell me. "I guess so," I reply respectfully.

"Is your dad inside?" he asks.

"Uh-hm. We can go in through the back kitchen door." I point to the open door across the parking lot.

Inside the kitchen, Dad looks half-eaten. The whole upper part of his body has disappeared inside the oven.

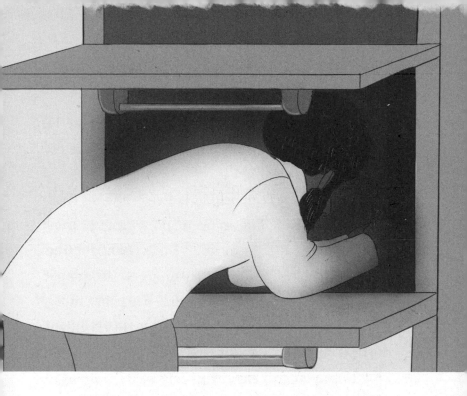

"Well, hello, cookie man," Mr. Reedy shouts. Dad immediately pulls his head from the oven's jaws.

"Ken! How are you, buddy?" Dad grabs Mr. Reedy's hand and gives it a good squeeze. "It's great to see you."

"You too." Mr. Reedy looks at the oven covered in black powdery soot. "What's happening here? You didn't burn your first batch, did you?"

I quickly change the subject. I want to leave before

Dad embarrasses me. "C'mon, Alex, I'll show you the rest of the store."

Dad's not having it. "That can wait, boys." He turns back to Mr. Reedy. "Ellis had a bit of...trouble...with the oven."

"Well, maybe I can help," Mr. Reedy offers. "I usually work on cars, but an oven and an engine aren't *that* different." Mr. Reedy grabs Dad's flashlight from the metal table. It immediately drops on the ground. "This dang Parkinson's," Mr. Reedy blurts in a mildly frustrated voice. Alex quickly picks up the flashlight, turns it on, and hands it to his dad.

"Here you go," says Alex. He sounds annoyed. Alex's dad annoys him a lot.

Mr. Reedy sticks the flashlight into the oven. His head follows inside. The flashlight shakes in Mr. Reedy's hand. The light bounces around the inside of the oven like a firefly. Mr. Reedy has had Parkinson's disease for a long time. It makes his whole body shake and twitch without wanting to. Alex's dad is really talented. He can fix anything. He used to repair cars until his hands got too shaky to do it anymore. He still tinkers with stuff for fun.

He also paints really big paintings. Mr. Reedy calls them "abstract," which means the paintings don't make a lot of sense. But they're super colorful.

From inside the oven, it sounds like a bunch of marbles rolling around in a metal sink. After a moment, Mr. Reedy pulls himself out. In the palm of his hand is a small brass box with three metal tubes sticking out of it. He holds it up for us to see.

"No wonder you had trouble," Mr. Reedy explains. "Not Ellis's fault at all. This thermometer is installed incorrectly, so the oven overheated. You're lucky the whole thing didn't go up in flames. I'm sure I have one of these in my garage. I'll get it replaced for you tomorrow. It might take me a little longer with these darn hands, but I won't charge you by the hour," he jokes.

"Ken, you're a lifesaver," Dad says gratefully. "I don't suppose you know how to fix a cracked mixing bowl, do you?" Dad points to the metal mixing bowl lying on its side.

"That's unusual, for a big bowl like this to crack. I might have some epoxy that can seal it. I'll see what I can find," Mr. Reedy says.

Back in the parking lot, Dad hands Mr. Reedy and Alex a small brown bag of cookies. "Here you go, guys. I made these at home earlier."

Mr. Reedy pulls a cookie from the bag and pops it in his mouth. "You are definitely onto something here. These are fabulous. Just what this neighborhood needs. A little sweetness."

As Mr. Reedy chews, he looks around the empty parking lot. Grandma still has some weeds to pull. Mr. Reedy is now walking around the parking lot. He lowers his head—like he's wandering on the beach looking for lost treasure. He walks to the far corner of the lot, turns around, and returns to Dad before asking him a question.

"Would you mind if I made you a little something? I have an idea you might like. Consider it a housewarming gift for the store."

Dad accepts. "Ken, I would be honored."

"Well, wait until you see it." Ken laughs. "Alright, boys, let's get home for dinner."

I'm a Man

After dinner, Alex and I head straight to his room.
We hang our sign on the door.

Alex has one plastic milk crate full of record albums—almost twenty in all. They actually belong to *both* of us, but we keep them at Alex's place because he has the only turntable. We're just getting started

with our collection. We pool our money to buy them from Tower Records. It's the greatest record shop in the world. One day, we'll have a whole room filled with records. Aside from my harmonica, these albums are the most important things I own.

As I thumb through them, the album covers fly past like a flip-book. I stop when I see the corner of one is bent. It's dog-eared like the pages of a book. I pull it from the crate and show it to Alex. Like I do every time. "You've gotta take better care of these."

"What's the big deal? It's just the cover. The album still plays," he says. Like he does every time. "Take it easy."

I would take it easy if Alex took better care of our collection. I slide the album out of its dog-eared cardboard cover and remove the shiny black vinyl from its paper sleeve. It's bigger than a dinner plate, with a small hole right in the center. As much as I love them, I actually wish albums were smaller. It would be cool if somehow you could take all of your favorite music with you—like in your pocket or something. I gently lay the album on the turntable. "Alex, you gotta take better care of our albums. Especially this one. It's totally dusty. You're gonna ruin it."

"What's the big deal?! Chill out. Just play it," Alex says, kicking a soccer ball against the wall.

I'm not *un*-chill. I just want Alex to take care of our albums. They are a big deal. I grab the bottom of my T-shirt, stretch it over the vinyl, and gently wipe off the dust. Then I lift the turntable arm ever so lightly. As it moves toward the album, the turntable starts spinning like a flying saucer. At the end of the turntable arm is a tiny needle. It's super small. I delicately hold it above the edge of the spinning vinyl. This is my favorite part of listening to albums. The drop. It's different from dropping cookie dough. This is the moment when that needle touches the vinyl and you hear the first sound. It's like turning on a light switch in a dark room. It feels like magic. If you drop the needle down too hard, it might skip the first note. If you

aim it wrong, you could miss the edge altogether. The needle drop requires total focus.

"Hurry up, Ellis," Alex shouts. He kicks the soccer ball against the wall for the fifth or sixth time, and his bedroom door flies open. Courtney stands there, in all of her nine-year-old rage.

"Stop! Kicking! The! Ball!" Courtney screams. Then she slams the door, ruining my needle drop. It bounces across the vinyl.

"Courtney!" I yell. "You ruined my drop. You made the needle skip!"

The door opens again. Courtney reappears. This time, she's all smiles. "Sorry, Ellis," she says sweetly. "I didn't see you there." She then gives Alex the stink eye before closing the door. Gently.

"God, she's the worst," Alex groans. "You're so lucky you don't have a sister. And what's up with her crush on you? It's so wrong." Alex kicks the soccer ball to the corner of the room, picks up the album cover, and sits on the edge of his bed. I pick up the needle and start again. Perfect drop. The song starts.

Now, when I was a young boy
At the age of five
My mother said I was gonna be
The greatest man alive

Muddy Waters's voice is booming through the speakers. He sounds old, but not like in a grandpa kind of way. He sounds like he knows things that *you* should know. He makes you want to pay attention to him—not because you're in trouble but because he just seems right. It's like he's a grown man who remembers what it's like to be a kid. He's serious but not angry. Muddy Waters sounds like he comes from a land far away. His voice is full of gravel. He's my very favorite singer of all time. He's the sound of the blues.

Blues is my favorite kind of music. Mom was the first person to play it for me. She told me that Africans brought it to America. It's kind of a secret language. Blues music can make me feel sad, but it also makes me feel stronger than the sadness. Blues singers beg, scream, and shout. They sound like nothing can scare them. They don't care what anyone thinks about them. It's also really easy to hear all of the instruments on blues records. There's usually just a singer, a guitar player, a drummer, a piano player, and a harmonica player. It sounds like they're all hanging out in a room together—like Alex and me.

I grab the album cover from Alex's hands. We sit next to each other studying every detail while I try and fix the dog-eared corner.

This album is called *The Real Folk Blues*. It has two photos of Muddy Waters. In one photo, his eyelids are heavy and his skin is dark and shiny like my dad's. He has a thin mustache above his lip—almost like it was drawn with a black marker. There's one big wrinkle across his forehead. It makes him look like he's worried. Muddy's eyes are closed in the other photo. His head is tilted toward the sky. It's almost like he's howling at the moon. Alex and I study every detail of the album cover while Muddy's voice thunders through the speakers.

> *But now I'm a man*
> *Way past twenty-one*
> *I want you to believe me, honey*
> *We having lots of fun*
> *I'm a man*
> *I spell M-*

Alex and I sing the rest of the words along with Muddy. "*A-N. That represents 'man.' No B-O-Y. That means 'mannish boy.' I'm a MAN.*" We both can't help but laugh with joy every time we hear Muddy Waters. He's so good. It doesn't sound like anything else.

Alex falls back on his bed staring up at the ceiling. Then he exhales. *"Man,* I wish I was Black."

"Um, what?" I reply.

Alex repeats the same five words. "I wish I was Black." He keeps talking while looking up at the ceiling. "Look at Muddy Waters. Look at almost everyone in our record collection. My favorite soccer player, Pelé. Even your dad. They're all just cooler."

"But those people aren't cool *because* they're Black. They're just cool. And my dad's definitely not as cool as yours. Your dad can paint and fix anything," I say.

"Not anymore," Alex corrects me. "Now that he has his Parkinson's, he's always…" Alex stops then continues. "He keeps making jokes about it, but it's not funny. He's sick. How can you joke when you're sick and can't even hold a flashlight? You're so lucky, Ellis."

"I get it," I say while examining *The Real Folk*

Blues. "That sucks about him being sick. But at least your dad *listens* to you. I bet he knows your birthday. And being the only Black kid in school isn't exactly cool. I get reminded of it every day. All these ridiculous questions like, 'Do you get tan in the summer?' 'I bet you dance really well, huh?' And everybody wants to touch my hair. 'Ooh, Ellis, your Afro is so funny. Why do you call it an Afro? Is that like *Afr*ica? Have you ever been to Africa?'"

Alex sits back up. "They're idiots. And I'll tell them next year at middle school. You should grow the biggest Afro you can." Alex grabs the album cover from my hand. "Then we can join Muddy Waters's band. We just need our own blues names."

Alex may not be right about my dad, but he's right about our names. All of the old blues players have cool names like Muddy Waters. There's lots of them: Slim Harpo, Little Walter, Lightnin' Hopkins, Junior Wells. Why did they change their names? Imagine just changing your name and reinventing yourself. One day you're one person, and the next day you're someone completely different. I wish I could do that.

A Bigger Bowl

The next day, Alex and I are sitting in the storage room of the cookie store. The fluorescent lights and linoleum floor make it look like an empty classroom. Soon it will be filled with ingredients for cookies—as soon as I can figure out the recipe.

"What about Muddy Ellis?" Alex asks.

"No way. There can only be one Muddy, and that's Muddy Waters. You've been thinking of names ever since we got here. Aren't you done? I've gotta figure out this recipe. Dad's making a big deal out of it."

I need to play some music so I can think. Grandma's note falls on the ground as I pull my harmonica from my pocket. Alex picks it up for me.

"'FITTT'? What is that?"

"My grandma. It's an acronym," I reply, grabbing the paper and stuffing it back in my pocket.

"Hey, do you know what SOS stands for?" Alex asks.

"Nope."

"'Save our ship,'" he says. "It's the only acronym I know."

"This one means family is tougher than time."

"Family is tougher than time? I don't get it."

"Don't worry about it," I say. "It's nothing."

Alex snaps his fingers. "How about Lightnin' Ellis?"

The storage room door opens before I have a chance to tell him how dumb that sounds. Dad guides the big mixing bowl into the room, rocking it from side to side. It has a big metal clamp attached to the edge.

"Hey, Dad, what kind of blues names should we give ourselves?"

"No time for that now, Little Man," he responds. I don't even know why I bothered to ask.

I shoot Alex a look. This is exactly what I was talking about last night. I wonder if he gets it now.

"Did my dad fix your bowl?" Alex asks.

"He sure did," Dad says. "He sealed the crack. We just have to let it sit for twenty-four hours." Dad settles the mixing bowl in the corner of the room. Then he looks up at me. "That gives us the rest of the day to figure out the recipe."

"Uh-huh," I mumble. I need to figure this out quickly. I really don't want to spend my whole day working on Dad's stupid recipe.

Dad turns to Alex. "Since your buddy is giving me the silent treatment, perhaps *you* can explain to him that we open for business in five weeks and six days. A cookie store needs cookies to sell. Remember what I said: fine-tune our recipe, get our ingredients, fix this store, and find our customers." Dad walks out of the room.

Why should I remember what he says? He won't even *listen* to what I say. I imitate Dad's bossy voice. "'A cookie store needs cookies to sell.'"

"I heard that, Ellis," Dad shoots back from the kitchen.

I lower my voice so only Alex can hear. "It's *his* dumb store. Let him fine-tune his own stupid recipe. And I hate Lightnin' Ellis, by the way."

"Alright, I'll keep thinking," Alex whispers back. "I don't know, Ellis, I think you can figure out this recipe thing." Alex looks at the mixing bowl. "But, man, that's a big bowl."

"It's beyond big!" I yell before lowering my voice again. "Dad's never made more than a few batches of cookies at once. This is the stupidest thing ever."

"I heard that, too, Ellis," Dad shoots back again.

"'I heard that, too,'" I mimic under my breath.

"What's the big deal?" Alex asks. "You can do this. You're really good at math. I don't know, I think it's kind of cool, Ellis. Your dad has a cookie store!" Alex looks around the empty storage room with the empty mixing bowl. He starts talking fast. Like he's trying to convince me. "I mean, he's *gonna* have a cookie store! And you're helping him! And I'm helping you! And that's kind of cool!"

"Will you please stop saying how cool this is?"

I beg Alex. "Look at this place. Nothing is cool about it."

I look at the mixing bowl in the corner of the storage room. The big metal clamp attached to the side makes it look like a giant teacup.

"Wait. I have an idea. Get in the bowl."

"What?" Alex asks.

"I'm gonna spin you in the mixing bowl," I tell him.

"No, you're not."

"Yes, I am," I insist. "Trust me. It'll be fun."

"Fun for who?" Alex asks. "You're always trying to get me to do dumb stuff."

"Just get in," I insist again. "Sometimes you gotta take a chance."

Alex pauses then says, "Okay." I can tell he's still not so sure. He steps into the bowl. The top of it comes to his knees. He tries to sit down but can't squeeze his butt down while his legs are inside the bowl. It starts to wobble. I quickly grab the side to hold it steady.

"You're too big," I say. "You have to sit down in it."

"I'm trying!"

I sigh. "Get out. I have another idea." Alex carefully steps out of the bowl while I hold it. "Okay, now *sit* in it instead of *stepping* in it," I tell him. "I'll hold the bowl."

Alex turns around. He sits his butt on the edge of the bowl while I hold the clamp on the opposite side. Then he slides backward inside. Alex looks like the letter *U*. His head at one side, his butt at the bottom, and feet at the top of the other side.

"Ellis, this isn't fun," Alex says nervously. "I think I'm stuck."

Alex tried to wriggle himself out. "I'm like ten times bigger than this bowl. I can't get out."

No way! That's it. "What did you say?" I ask Alex.

"I can't get out." Alex says again. This time more nervously.

"No, the other part."

"There is no other part! I'm stuck!" Alex yells. "Why do you always make me do dumb stuff?"

"I didn't put you in the bowl. I just *asked* you to get in the bowl," I correct him.

"Whatever. Now get me out!"

"Hold on a minute. I think I have it."

"Have WHAT?" Alex exclaims.

Dad thunders back into the storage room. He doesn't like what he sees. "What is going on here?" He reaches over and grabs Alex's wrists. Dad pulls him out of the bowl. Alex's U-shaped body is now standing straight up. I hide my harmonica in my back pocket. There's no way I'm letting Dad grab it again.

"Does somebody want to explain what's happening here?" Dad asks us.

Alex freezes. "Uh...uh...," he stammers.

"Yes?" Dad waits for an answer.

Alex tries to get out an answer. "Ellis...he...I mean, we...wanted to...spin..."

Dad is shocked. "Spin?!?"

I need to change the subject. Fast. I think I know what to say to get Dad's attention. I quickly check my brain. I want to make sure this is worth saying out loud. Yep. I'm sure.

"Dad, I figured it out. I know how to fix the recipe."

A Fine-Tuned Recipe

Dad is confused. I can tell by the way his eyes are squeezing closer together. I point to the large metal mixing bowl. "This mixing bowl is ten times bigger than yours!" Before Dad can answer or take my harmonica, I run out of the storage room and quickly return with his chipped ceramic mixing bowl. I place it inside of the metal one.

"Look," I say, pointing inside. "You could fit ten of your bowls inside this big one. That's the answer to the recipe." Alex and Dad both look at me like I'm a stranger. They don't get it.

"It's a *conversion factor*," I explain. "I learned it in my fifth-grade chemistry class this year. It was actually kinda cool." What I am NOT saying is that I learned it from Brad Katz, who sat in front of me. He took really good notes in class. He's also the only kid on earth shorter than me. Sometimes when I was in a bind, I'd look over his shoulder to figure out what I missed. I'm not proud of this.

I continue explaining. "A conversion factor is how you change the amount of something into a *different* amount of something." I'm trying to remember the formula Brad wrote on his quiz. It's the one that got me an A+. I should have thanked him. Man, I hope there's another Brad Katz in middle school.

I search my brain again. What was it...? Oh yeah, I remember! Before it escapes my brain, I ask Alex to get me a pen.

"*Please.*" Dad reminds me of my manners.

"Please," I add, rolling my eyes.

Alex quickly returns with a pen. I write down Brad's formula from our A+ quiz.

$$\frac{\text{New Yield}}{\text{Old Yield}} = \text{Conversion Factor}$$

I point to the top line on the left. "*Yield* is a fancy word for 'amount.' It's how much of something you *want*." I then point to the line below. "And this is how much of something you *have*." Alex has a blank look on his face.

"I'm already confused," he says.

I continue writing on the paper. Hopefully, Alex will get it. "It's actually not that confusing. Dad's current recipe fills his ceramic bowl with batter. But we need ten ceramic bowls of batter to fill this big metal one. So, we divide one into ten. That gives us a conversion factor of ten."

"Basically, if we want enough batter to fill this bowl, we need to multiply each ingredient by ten," Dad answers. "I get it. Good job, Little Man. You just fine-tuned our recipe. I should have thought of that. I guess math isn't so dumb after all. Who knew?" Dad gives me a wink.

No way. Dad knew how to do this all along? Is

this his idea of summer school or something? I am not getting pranked by my own dad. Let him deal with the other items on his list by himself. I'm done.

Dad continues. "Alright, I'm going to convert the ingredients—*and* I'm going to forget what I saw with this mixing bowl. This time. Now, let's get to fixing this store. I want you boys to start pulling up that old carpet out front. Someone is coming to lay some nice new wooden floors. The wood is gonna give this place a real vibe." Dad disappears into the kitchen.

If Dad's such a math genius, why can't he pull up his own carpet? Ugh, I can't believe I have to touch it.

Alex and I look down at the littered sea of orange shag below us. "It's like walking in a sandbox made of cigarette butts," he says.

"I know," I say, nodding in agreement. "It's disgusting." I stare at the carpet. It's tightly tucked into every corner of the store.

"How are we gonna rip this up?" Alex wonders.

"We just need to pull really hard. C'mon, let's get this over with as quick as we can." I'm done helping my dad.

I lead Alex to the corner of the room. We both grab the edge of the carpet where it meets the wall. "On the count of three. One. Two. THREE!" We pull. Hard. A little too hard. The carpet breaks away from the floor and sends us flying backward across the room. We land on our backs. A cloud of dust engulfs us. Our heads are covered in cigarette ash. Alex starts coughing. Hard. He looks like a cat trying to hack up a fur ball. I feel I might choke to death. THIS is the way it ends. Suffocating in an orange shag sea of cigarettes. I pull my shirt up over my mouth and nose, leaving only my eyes visible. Through the ashy snowfall, I see Alex's furball cough turn into a full-blown laugh.

"Your head. It looks like it's vanishing."

I hold on to the neck of my shirt and slowly sink the rest of my head down. From inside my shirt, I call out, "Alex! There is a ghost among us. The headless ghost of Hollywood! Beware of the orange carpet!"

I pop my head back through my shirt just as a man

walks inside the store. Through the fading dust cloud I can see him wobbling—like he's trying to keep from falling off a balance beam. Alex and I sit straight up.

"What the hell is going on in here?" the man slurs angrily. Alex and I can smell his breath drifting across the room. He's totally drunk. Dark crud is caked on his clothes. It looks like he took a shower in a school bus exhaust pipe. Alex and I are frozen. We've never been this close to anyone who looks like they might pass out or punch us.

"We're opening a store selling chocolate chip cookies." Dad appears out of nowhere and steps in front of us. Alex and I exhale at the same time. Dad glares stone-faced at the drunk who sways back and forth like...well...like a drunk. Slowly, his eyes fall shut. I look up at Dad above me. Then I look at the drunk. Is he asleep?

Without warning, the drunk's eyes snap back open. He nearly falls over before stepping forward three times to catch himself. His filthy foot lands right next to my pinky finger. The drunk slowly rises up and looks at my dad like he's angry at him about something.

"Coons? Selling cookies? Ha!" The drunk spits on the carpet, stumbles around, and wobbles out of the store down Sunset Boulevard.

Alex, Dad, and I all hold our breath. Dad soon exhales. If he's breathing, I guess we can, too. Alex and I let out big sighs. Dad helps us to our feet then locks the door.

"What does that mean, Dad?" I ask. "*Coon*."

Dad turns around. He looks like he did in the

Rock and Roll Ralphs yesterday. Like he's caught in a daydream. But not a happy one.

"It's nothing. It's just a drunk man talkin' non-sense." Dad makes his way back to the kitchen. "You boys get the rest of that carpet up."

Alex and I stare out the front door.

"Do you think he'll come back?" I ask.

"I hope not," Alex wishes. Then he adds, "Hey, Ellis?"

"Yeah," I say. My eyes are fixed on the door. I can hear Alex clear his throat.

"I know what that word means."

Keeping It Real Always

Alex and I sit silently in the middle of the store. We're still in shock. I softly blow my harmonica. That drunk's voice is still in my head. *Coon.* He said it like it was some dirty animal.

"That word is like the N-word," Alex explains. "My uncle said it at our house once. My dad kicked him out."

I don't understand why Dad said it was nothing. I climb down the mountain of carpet and march into the kitchen. Dad is measuring chocolate chips. I take a deep breath.

"Dad, I want to know what that word means."

Dad looks up. He takes his own deep breath. He looks like I do when I'm trying to decide whether or not I should lie about something. Alex pokes his head into the kitchen. He wants to hear this, too.

"Have you ever insulted someone at school?" Dad asks.

"I don't know. Maybe," I mumble. I'm not sure if I want Dad to know about the time I called Amanda Freeman a pig face.

Dad wrinkles his forehead. His eyes squeeze shut. He pinches the bridge of his nose. He looks like he's trying to remember something or forget it. "That word is an insult, Ellis. Said by bullies who want to scare you. People who think they are better than us." Dad opens his eyes. He stares at Alex and me. "We are not bullies. And we will not be scared by bullies. You hear me?"

"Yes, Dad," I reply. I need to apologize to Amanda if I ever see her again.

Dad looks through the kitchen door at the mound of orange carpet we pulled up. His face suddenly changes like he's seen a ghost. "Man, I don't believe this," Dad says, shaking his head. "He finally showed up."

Dad unlocks the front door, letting a man inside. It's not the drunk bully. *This* man looks like he just landed from outer space. He's wearing a dashiki. Only this one is super long. It hangs to his ankles, which are laced in leather straps from the sandals on his wide feet.

"Wow, your Afro!" I say out loud before I can get the words back in my mouth. This man's Afro is huge. It's perfectly round. I've never seen an Afro like this one. It must take him all morning to comb it. The man looks down at me. He flashes a blinding smile.

"Thank you, Big Brother. My hair is my pride and my strength. You got yourself a good start there," he says, gently patting my hair. He turns to Dad. "Pops, aren't you going to introduce me?"

"Ellis, meet…" But before Dad can finish his sentence, the Afroed stranger grabs my hand and greets me himself. "DJ Wishbone—Keeping. It. Real. Always. K.I.R.A." He says *K-I-R-A* like he is counting—slapping a different part of my hand on each letter. It feels like I've been given *his* secret handshake. I didn't even know adults had secret handshakes. DJ Wishbone seems like he has lots of secrets. I feel nervous and excited around him at the same time.

"DJ Wishbone?" Dad asks. "That's your name these days?"

"At your service, Pops," DJ Wishbone says proudly. "You been listening to my show?"

"No, I've been a little busy," Dad replies. Then he says to me, "Ellis, uh…Wishbone…is someone I've known a long time. I also hear he's the new host of the afternoon radio show on KIRA. The radio station down the street."

"That is the truth," Wishbone declares. "I've been on the air for two months. When are you going to stop by the radio station, Pops? We're finally neighbors. It's almost like the old days."

Honestly, I can't tell if Dad and Wishbone like each other or hate each other.

"How long until we get some cookies, Pops?" Wishbone asks, looking around the empty store. Dad points to the sign on the door.

"Want me to show you around, Mr. Wishbone?" I offer.

"I'd love that, Big Brother. But I need to get on the air. My show starts in less than an hour. I just dropped in here to see what was shaking. Whadda you say, Pops? Let Big Brother come down to the station? I'll take care of him."

"Please, Dad?" I beg. Hanging out in a radio station?

That's got to be the coolest thing ever. I can't even imagine how many albums are inside a radio station.

"Maybe next time," Dad says, shooting me down. "Right now, we need to fix this store."

Wishbone takes a step back. "That's cool, Pops. Catch you on the flip." He looks down at me and says, "I'm just down the block when you're ready for the funk."

Wishbone walks out and heads down to the edge of Sunset Boulevard. Alex and I turn to Dad, waiting for some kind of explanation. Who *is* he? Where does he come from? And what is the funk? We wait. And wait. Nothing. Dad doesn't say a thing. Alex breaks the silence.

"How did you meet Wishbone, Mr. Johnson?"

Dad locks the door and goes back into the kitchen. "Not now, Alex."

All Dad says is "It's nothing" and "Not now." That's it. Alex and I will have to find out about Wishbone on our own.

"I don't know about you, Ellis," Alex says. "But I think I'm ready for the funk!"

I'm definitely ready. I just wish I knew what it was.

The Divorced Dads Bungalow

Dad's Rambler stops in front of Alex's house. All three of us are sitting up front on the bench seat. I begged Dad to let me sleep over at the Reedys' again. He told me I can't spend every night there. I don't know why. I hate staying at my dad's apartment. It's awful. It's so bad that I would rather stay at Grandma's place. But that would never happen. Grandma always says, "I don't want no smelly boys gettin' in all of my business. I keep to myself."

Alex slides across the seat and gets out of the car. He sticks his hand back through the half-open window. One palm slap, two fist bumps, then grab pinky fingers.

"Catch you on the flip, Ellis," Alex says. "Thanks, Mr. Johnson."

"We'll see you back at the store soon," Dad promises.

Not soon enough.

The Rambler pulls away from the curb. I look at Alex waving goodbye through the side-view mirror. Man, this is going to be a long night.

Dad's apartment building is about twenty minutes from Mom's house. But twenty minutes in Hollywood is a LONG distance. Technically, Dad's place is called a *bungalow*. I guess that means it's a really small house. There are four bungalows all clumped together. They look like cabins. A sad little garden sits in the middle of all of them. Whoever built this place must have thought a garden would make it less sad looking. They were wrong. All of the bungalow windows have bars covering them. As Dad unlocks his door, another man walks out of his bungalow, across the sad garden. He shuts his door and locks it before glancing over and smiling.

"Got your kid for the night?" he asks, knowing the answer. "I'm on my way to pick up mine. A little mischief time with Dad. One week on, one week off. Have fun!"

Oh, did I mention that everyone who lives here is a divorced dad? It's like summer camp for divorced dads. The door opens, and Dad turns on the light. It's just like I remember it from my last sleepover. The lime green carpet is almost as ugly as the store's old orange shag. It's cleaner, though. One thing I'll say about Dad is that he's clean. Everything is in its place.

"I got your room all ready for you," Dad says. My "room" is the sofa bed pulled out into the middle of the living room. Dad's room is behind the closed door. The bathroom is in there, too. I sit on the bed cross-legged, quickly adjusting when a mattress spring pokes me in the butt.

Dad throws down his leather shoulder bag and opens the fridge. "Let's see what we have for dinner."

Nothing. Of course. The refrigerator is empty

except for three navel oranges, a bottle of Vernors ginger ale, and a carton of eggs. Aside from cookies, Dad doesn't really make much. I doubt *anyone* makes dinner in the Divorced Dad Bungalows. Dad closes the refrigerator and claps his hands together. Here we go. This happened the last two times I slept over. Dad acts like he's going to cook dinner, he opens the refrigerator, realizes there's nothing to cook, claps his hands, and announces...

"We're having dinner at Tiny Naylor's!"

Tiny Naylor's is not your typical restaurant. It's a drive-in restaurant. You get to eat dinner in your car. In fact, cars are parked around the restaurant in a big circle. All of them are covered under a large slanted canopy. It looks like all of the parked cars are sitting under the wings of a huge bird preparing to fly. Straight ahead through the window of the restaurant kitchen, I can see "Tiny." He's the owner. He's actually not tiny at all. He weighs three hundred pounds. That's just a guess. But trust me, he's big, not tiny.

A waitress attaches a tray to Dad's side of the car. She has electric red hair. She looks like she belongs in an old black-and-white movie. Her name tag says RUTH. I try rolling down my window, but it gets stuck halfway like it always does.

"Why don't you roll down the *back* window, sweetie?" Ruth suggests. "I'll attach the tray back there, and you can reach over the front seat for your food." That's a good idea. I roll down the back window. The redheaded waitress attaches my tray and winks at me. "Where there's a will, there's a way."

Dad bites into his patty melt. A string of Swiss cheese gets caught in his beard. I immediately reach for the curly fries.

The sound of Dad's chewing fills the car. Mom says he smacks his food. It drives her crazy. I automatically turn to do Mom's work for her.

"Dad…"

"What's up?" Dad says with a mouthful of patty melt.

I almost tell him to stop but decide against it. "Never mind." Smacking food in your own car should be allowed. Besides, I realize I was just smacking my curly fries.

Dad and I start slurping our milkshakes when we hear three short car horn beeps next to us. Through Dad's open window, I see the Divorced Bungalow Dad wave to us. His son sits next to him sheepishly.

"Hey, guys!" he says, wiping his face with a napkin. "Look at us. Mischief time with dads. Feels good, right?"

"Uh…sure does," Dad says. Then he turns to me and whispers, "As Grandma would say, this fool better *git*. You think he's gonna talk to us all night from over there?"

I laugh and grab another handful of curly fries. "I don't know. They might want to eat in the back of the car with us."

"Hey, don't talk with curly fries in your mouth. It's rude." Dad's only kidding this time. He puts his arm around me and gives me a squeeze just as Ruth the waitress brings us the check.

"Now that's a pretty picture," she says, looking at us. "You two stay out of trouble, now."

Back at the bungalow, Dad and I each brush our teeth with one hand and hold our stomachs with the other. I walk through Dad's bedroom and hop onto the sofa bed, tucking myself tightly between two loose springs. Dad kisses my forehead.

"'Night, Little Man," he says. "Rest up. We have a big day tomorrow." I can hear Dad's stomach grumbling. He rubs it. "Man, that milkshake is making my stomach feel funky."

"Is that what Wishbone meant?" I ask Dad.

Dad takes a second to remember what I'm talking about. "No, this definitely is *not* the same funk. There is a big difference between *feeling* funky and *getting* funky."

Man, the funk is complicated. "Dad, I'd really like to visit Wishbone at his radio station. Can I, *pleeeeasse*?"

"We'll see, Little Man," Dad says. That probably means no. "Now, rest!"

The bedroom door closes. Lying on the sofa bed in the dark, I think about Dad at Aunt Della's. Is this what he felt like? He said he was so happy sleeping on her sofa bed. But I miss my own bed, and waking up with Mom *and* Dad in the house. I wonder how Mom is doing with her "me time." I can hear my stomach gurgling. I lie on my right side, my left side. I can't get comfortable. Plus, every time I move, the bed squeaks. I could use some earplugs.

From the other side of the door, I hear Dad's voice. "That's a whole lotta squeaking out there. Your stomach feeling funky, too?"

"Yeah, I think the milkshakes may have been too much."

Dad opens the door and invites me inside. "C'mon and get in bed with me."

No argument from me. I grab my pillow, slide over the broken mattress springs, and slip into bed next to Dad. We lie side by side. His foot touches mine under the covers. Our stomachs are gurgling. I hear the bathroom faucet dripping into the sink.

"I gotta call the landlord about that faucet," Dad whispers.

"I don't know, I kinda like it. It has the same beat as that Muddy Waters song." I sing along to the water drip under my breath.

Now, when I was a young boy
[Drip, drip. Drip, drip.]
At the age of five
[Drip, drip. Drip, drip.]

To my total surprise, Dad sings the next two lines.

My mother said I was gonna be
[Drip, drip. Drip, drip.]
The greatest man alive

Then we both sing the best part together.

I'm a man
[Drip, drip. Drip, drip.]
I spell M-

"Dad, you know about Muddy Waters?"

"King of the blues," Dad says.

"What's your favorite Muddy Waters song?"

Dad turns over. "Not now. Time to sleep."

Of course. He can't even talk to me about Muddy Waters. Still, I gotta admit, even though my stomach is gurgling, I really love eating in the car at the drive-in. I hope Tiny Naylor's never goes away.

Walking with Wishbone

Our Rambler parks in front of the store. I don't see Grandma's white Cadillac.

"Where's Grandma, Dad?"

"She's visiting some plant nurseries. You know Grandma and her plants. She'll be here later. There's still weeds waiting for her."

Dad gets out and unlocks the front door. I step onto the sidewalk and sigh. It still doesn't look like any kind of store from the outside. This place needs a lot more fixing. The mountain of orange carpet greets us inside, rolled up like a giant sausage. Dad claps his hands—the same way Coach Brossy does at school when he's trying to get us excited about doing push-ups. I'm never excited to do push-ups. Somehow, I don't think I'm going to be excited about what Dad has planned today.

"Alright!" Dad announces. "We've got carpet to move and no time to lose."

Yep. Not excited.

Dad cuts two pieces from the carpet mound. He shoves one underneath each front door so they stay open. We stand side by side facing the orange mountain. Then, walking backward, we drag the carpet toward the front door.

"Use your legs," Dad says. That's also what Coach Brossy says during gym class. I walk slowly in reverse—one small step at a time. This carpet is HEAVY. We get through the front doors and step onto Sunset. Another step back then...*BAM!*

I back right into Wishbone. He's dressed exactly the same as yesterday. Did he stay out all night just roaming around Hollywood? Wishbone looks at the giant roll of carpet lying on Sunset Boulevard.

"You two rolling out the red carpet for your customers?" he asks jokingly.

Dad is not amused. "It's a cookie store, not a nightclub."

"You got that right, Pops," Wishbone says. "No one needs to be messing around with no nightclubs. Ain't that right?"

"Yeah, that's right," Dad says, giving Wishbone a side-eye.

I get the feeling they are talking about something specific. They sound like they're arguing even though they're not. It's funny...Wishbone and Dad kind of remind me of Mom and Dad. Mom and Dad always have three kinds of arguments. The *first* kind is when they just yell at each other. Those are the worst. The *second* kind of argument is when they correct each other about stuff—like Mom telling Dad to stop smacking his food. The *third* kind of argument is when they bring up something from the past. They each talk about it completely differently—like they each read a different book. *This* is the kind of arguing Dad and Wishbone are having now. They haven't read the same book.

It's time to see if I can change the subject. "Mr. Wishbone, I think I'm ready for the funk," I blurt out.

Dad and Wishbone fall silent. They look at each other. I look at them. We all wait for someone to say something. Finally, Wishbone goes first.

"Well, well." Wishbone smiles slyly. "Big Brother wants to get funky. What do you say, Pops?"

Dad scratches his beard. He always scratches his beard when he's thinking. That's a good sign. It's *way* better than "We'll see." He scratches again. He looks at Wishbone. I look at him. We both wait for Dad to say something. Finally, Dad lets his hand fall and exhales.

"Don't think this is anything but a field trip," he tells Wishbone. "This don't change a thing."

Wishbone nods slowly. "It ain't nothing *but* a thing."

I'm confused. Does this mean I can go to the radio station?

"One hour," Dad says. "No detours. No distractions."

"Promise," I say.

Dad gives Wishbone a look that is awfully close to Mrs. Cook's stink eye. "Keep it cool with my little man," he says.

"I'm always cool, Pops," Wishbone says. Then he puts his arm across me as we head east down Sunset.

Wishbone and I walk past the empty stores. A plastic bag blows by my ankles. A city bus stops for an elderly man. A police car zigzags through traffic, the siren so loud that I have to cover my ears.

"Man, I hope your pops' cookie store can turn this block around," Wishbone says. "This neighborhood could use some brotherly love."

He's right. Anyone can see this block needs some attention. But walking with Wishbone, it doesn't seem scary anymore. It's weird how things can look so dangerous when really, they're just different. Maybe Dad's store *could* turn this block around. I mean, if a cookie store can't brighten up a block, then what can?

"Mr. Wishbone?" I ask.

"Call me Wishbone, Big Brother."

Wow. That's the first time an adult has ever told me to drop the *mister*.

"Okay," I say before trying it out. "Wishbone... do you think I could get my Afro like yours?"

Sticking out of the top of Wishbone's Afro is a small fist. It's not a real one. It's plastic. The plastic fist is at the end of a handle attached to a metal comb. The comb has about a dozen narrow teeth. I can only see a little bit of them before they disappear into a dark Afro sea. Wishbone grabs the plastic fist with his right hand. In one move, he pulls it out of his hair and sticks it into mine.

"You can have any kind of Afro you want," Wishbone tells me.

We arrive at the edge of Sunset Boulevard in front of a building pulsating with music. At the top of the chipped cement stairs is a glass door. It's tinted like the windows of a limousine. White letters are stuck on the front of it. Some of them are peeling off.

A man emerges from inside. As he opens the door, some of the music escapes, following him down the stairs. Then the door quickly shuts, trapping the rest of the music back inside. The man gives Wishbone a fist bump as he reaches the bottom of the steps.

"'Sup, 'Bone," he says in a cool whisper.

"My man," Wishbone replies. They sound like they are speaking in a secret language.

The building looks like it might burst open from the music inside. My foot is tapping to the beat. "'Sup," I say to myself quietly. It doesn't sound the same when I say it. I'll keep practicing.

I follow Wishbone up the stairs. He holds the door open then whisks me inside. Everyone's clothes and hair are fantastic, just like Wishbone's.

They all look like they've reinvented themselves. I've never seen this many Black people in real life. Every Black person in Hollywood must be in this building. Everyone looks like me. It feels like a long-lost family reunion with the best music ever. *This* is where I want to be.

Don't Fight the Funk

Welcome to the mothership, Big Brother. Make yourself at home." Wishbone removes his pitch-black sunglasses for the first time. His eyes are warm and a bit yellowish and sleepy. He leads me into his DJ booth. It's a small windowless box the size of my bedroom. And the walls are totally covered with shelves of records. This is the largest record collection I've ever seen besides Tower Records.

My eyes move up the rows of albums and land on the ceiling. "Whoa!" I say, staring above me. "I've never seen that before." The entire ceiling is covered with posters and stickers. Wishbone looks up like he's gazing at the stars at night.

"You're looking at my Musical Constellation of Blackness." He speaks like a preacher.

"Your what?"

"Those are brothers and sisters who shake your booty and move your mind!" he shouts. It still doesn't make much sense. But it seems to make TOTAL sense to Wishbone. The posters are filled with futuristic band names. Some of them I remember seeing in the record bin: Kool & the Gang, Fatback Band, and Funkadelic. Man, I wish Alex was here to see this.

In the center of the room, Wishbone sits at a short L-shaped counter. He pulls a pair of headphones into his Afro and over his ears. Then he waves his hand toward an empty chair across from him. I sit down, my feet barely touching the ground. I'm afraid to make a move or touch anything. This is the most epic moment of my life. I don't want to ruin it. How does someone this cool know my dad? Dad doesn't know *anyone* who's cool. A second pair of headphones looks up at me from the countertop.

"Go on," Wishbone says. I put the headphones over my ears as Wishbone pulls a microphone toward him. It's attached to the end of a mechanical arm. Wishbone speaks smoothly into the microphone. His voice sounds like it's coming from inside my head. A sign above the door lights up red. I read the words: ON AIR.

"Greetings, brothers and sisters. This is DJ Wishbone at your musical service. Keeping. It. Real. *Always*. We're gonna start things off with some cool funk for this hot Friday. This is a Funkadelic jam called 'Can You Get to That.'" Wishbone lowers the arm of a turntable. The needle touches the edge of the black vinyl. It's a perfect needle drop. He makes it look so easy. Wishbone's voice is replaced with a slippery acoustic guitar sliding around inside my brain. A hi-hat cymbal announces the arrival of a rumbling bass. Now the guitar, bass, and drums sound like they are twisting around each other in circles. The sound is loud and strange. It sounds like another world. The instruments rumble in my ears and pound my chest. I instantly rip off my headphones.

"Ooh! The funk got ya!" Wishbone yells. "It'll do that every time." Wishbone switches off the ON AIR sign. He then turns a big black knob on his desk. Instantly, the room is filled with music. Wishbone takes off his headphones, and pretends like he's playing guitar while his mouth makes a rubber band sound. He's making the same notes as the Funkadelic song. "Big Brother is getting funky. It got ya. The groove. The GROOVE! The groove is too strong! It's that deep pocket. You CAN'T resist it!" He slowly rises from his chair. His gold chain is swinging side to side. It's dancing to the groove. I can't help but laugh. Wishbone pulls me onto my feet.

"C'mon, Big Brother!" Wishbone tells me. "You need to chill. Like your pops. Now can you get to *that*?" Wishbone shakes an invisible Hula-Hoop around his hips. His gold chain nearly smacks his face. He leans down really close while making his rubber band sound with his mouth. He then spins and dances himself around the L-shaped counter. I follow him before I can even think about how stupid I must look.

"Feel your body, Big Brother," Wishbone says, looking over his shoulder at me. "Get in the pocket. Shake that thing. Don't fight the funk."

"I think I got the funk!" I say, laughing. Actually, I might *really* have the funk. My body is moving in ways that must look SO dumb, but it's really fun. "Check this out," I warn. I'm gonna do it. I'm gonna get to that.

Wishbone nods his approval. Here comes the funk. One hundred percent pure...

...darkness. The music has stopped. All of the lights are out. Wishbone's DJ booth has turned into a cave.

"Man, that funk was too much." Wishbone sighs. "We've got a problem, Big Brother. I am not proud to give you this piece of information. However, you should know: I am very afraid of the dark."

Huh? If he's afraid, should *I* be afraid? "Wishbone, what do we do?" I ask, trying to keep calm—which really isn't that hard to do. It's just a dark room.

Wishbone answers. He doesn't sound very calm. "Step outside the mothership, Big Brother.

Ask someone for a flashlight. My batteries died. Man. I should've replaced them when the power went down yesterday."

"Yesterday?" I say in disbelief. "How often do you lose the power?"

"At least once a day," Wishbone tells me. "The whole block has a problem. Now get that flashlight before I start sweating through my dashiki."

Standing in the dark hallway of KIRA Radio, I place my hands against the wall to guide me toward the front. At the end of the hallway, a woman wearing braids is sitting behind a desk. Her face glows from the flashing buttons on the large telephone in front of her. The phone lights and buzzes like an arcade video game.

"Excuse me—"

The braided woman interrupts without missing a beat. "Here you go, honey." She hands me a flashlight. "You better get back to the mothership. Wishbone does not like being in the dark."

"Yep. He told me," I say. "Thank you." I take the

flashlight. I turn it on and return to rescue Wishbone, making my way back down the hallway. The beam from my flashlight hits the glitter on the carpet. It looks like the Milky Way under my feet. I reach the door of the mothership. I pull it open. It's heavy. I have to stick the flashlight in my pocket so I can use both arms to tug at it. The door seals shut behind me just as I step inside and the lights suddenly turn back on.

"Brothers and sisters, let there be LIGHT," I hear. Wishbone and his giant Afro are squeezed underneath the L-shaped counter. He breathes a sigh of relief and uncorks himself from the tiny space before yanking himself into his chair. Wishbone then grabs his microphone and says calmly, "My apologies for steppin' on our groove. But we've got the power runnin' and more funk comin'. This is fifteen-year-old Michael Jackson and his brothers. The Jackson 5 singing 'Get It Together.'" Wishbone announces the song then drops the needle again.

Hey, it's just like Grandma says. Get It Together. G.I.T. "It's got a strong groove," I tell Wishbone. I'm pretty sure I know what I'm talking about now.

"Indeed it do, Big Brother. Indeed it do," Wishbone confirms. "It's that Motown sound." He points to the word *Motown* in the corner of the Jackson 5 record album cover. I see the words "The Sound of Young America" on it.

"My friend Alex and I like to play albums," I say.

Wishbone flashes his brilliant smile. "I knew there was a reason I liked you. Keep spinning those records. Do it before the future comes." Wishbone looks up at his Musical Constellation of Blackness. He scans the albums lining his walls. "I'll tell you, Big Brother. Someday all this music is gonna be up in the clouds."

That sounds pretty weird. Music in the clouds?

"It's science fiction, my man." Wishbone stares at the ceiling like it's the sky. "We'll just say the name of a song out loud and it'll play." Wishbone then yells up at the ceiling, "Hey, Cece, play the Jackson 5!"

"Who's Cece?" I ask.

"She's the lady in the clouds playing me any song I want," Wishbone answers. He almost makes it sound real.

I then ask the most important question I have. "Wishbone, how did you and my dad meet?"

Wishbone keeps staring at Cece in the sky. Without looking down, he replies, "You'll have to ask your pops about that." Then he chuckles to himself and says, "Tell him you want to know about the Rat Trap."

A Sugar Storm

Wishbone walks me to the bottom of the KIRA stairs. I can feel his long fingers on my shoulders as he points me west down Sunset Boulevard. "Your pops is waitin' for you," Wishbone calls as he struts back up the stairs. "You help him get those cookies ready." Then the front door opens, releasing the funk inside. It's so loud I can hardly hear him as he says goodbye. "Catch you on the flip, Big Brother." And just like that, Wishbone is sucked inside. Both he and the funk disappear. Man, radio stations are strange. I can't wait to go back.

I pull out my harmonica and head back to the cookie shop. I can see Dad in the distance, watching me from the sidewalk. I search for notes on my harmonica. The ones that match that Funkadelic song. By the time I reach Dad, I have it figured out. I'm playing the notes in circles.

"Ahh, I see Wishbone gave you a little Black Power," Dad remarks, seeing the fist pick sticking out of my Afro. "Well, come on in, Funky Harmonica Player. I've got a surprise for you."

Back inside the store, Dad stands by the closed storage room door. He grins and asks, "Are you ready?" I nod and put my harmonica in my pocket. Dad pushes the door open.

I can't believe my eyes. The room is bulging with huge sacks of sugar and flour. Each pile is three times taller than me. Only a couple of feet separate each stack. They feel as tall as the avocado trees in my backyard.

"Now that we fine-tuned the recipe, it's time to get our ingredients." There goes Dad and his list again. "This is a start. I'm still having a hard time finding chocolate chips. I hope the Rock and Roll Ralphs gets more soon, to keep us stocked until we find a supplier."

"Dad, can I make this room a clubhouse?" I ask without knowing if I should. I mean, this *would* be the best clubhouse ever. I can hang posters on the ceiling. Maybe Alex will bring his record player. I bet we could make it as cool as Wishbone's mothership.

Dad scratches his beard. That's a good sign. After a few more beard scratches, he breaks his silence. "Okay. Go for it. If you don't mind a clubhouse filled with chocolate chip cookie ingredients. But I need everything kept safe in there. No messing with those bags."

"Thanks, Dad. This is gonna be great."

"You're welcome, Little Man. Just be careful of these sacks. Each one weighs fifty pounds. You could get seriously hurt if one falls on you." Dad reaches his hand behind one of the stacks of sugar. "Oh, I got you something." Dad hands me a baseball glove. It's shiny and smells like a new pair of shoes. "I remember how you wanted to play in the World Series. Thanks for helping with the recipe 'conversion factor.'"

"Uh...Dad, I don't play baseball anymore."

The last time I played was a tee-ball tournament in first grade. I barely remember it. Dad was late as usual.

Dad swallows hard. "Well, I guess I got that wrong," he replies. He lowers his head and leaves the storage room. I lay the glove on the floor. Maybe I'll give it to Alex. The smell of sugar tickles the inside of my nose. I breathe out and slowly walk into the sugary forest. After taking a few steps, I look up at two stacks of sugar towering over both sides of me. Each tan-colored bag is stitched shut with a thick piece of string. I read the blue words printed on the side.

PURE CANE SUGAR FROM HAWAII

I close my eyes, imagining I'm stranded at the bottom of a tall sugar canyon. If I have any chance of being resuced, I need to climb to the top. I can almost feel the sugar hitting my face—like I'm under a waterfall. Wait a minute! Sugar *is* hitting my face. My eyes open. The word *CANE* comes into focus on the side of a bag. A slow stream of sugar is pouring out of a small hole in the letter *A*—like a steady, dripping faucet.

I can fix this. This is my chance to make up for the chocolate chip disaster. And the oven disaster. And whatever else might happen next. I've gotta keep these bags safe like Dad asked. I wipe the sugar and sweat from my face then carefully place my feet on the edges of the bags near the bottom of the canyon. One on the left. The other on the right. Now I need to pull myself up. Pushing down on my forearms, I hold myself up with my hands then release my feet. My legs are now dangling just above the ground. It's kinda like Coach Brossy's gym class. Okay, it's time for stomach crunches. I pull my knees to my belly and land my feet on the row of bags under my hands. That's it. I've got this. After a few more sugar pull-ups, I'm halfway up the canyon about five feet above the ground. The small hole is within reach. I rub my finger gently on the letter *A*.

Uh-oh...

My finger poked right through the bag. The hole is now twice as big. All of this sugar is going to flood the floor. Think fast, Ellis. Quickly, I open my mouth underneath the faucet of sugar while plant-ing the palm of my hand over the hole. It worked. No more sugar flowing. I can easily clean up the small amount on the floor. This will work out...as long as I keep my hand on this hole. Or move my hand and eat all of the sugar before it hits the floor. How long would it take to eat fifty pounds of sugar?

I can feel the sweat beading up on my forehead again. Keep thinking, Ellis. Okay, I've got another idea. I'll plug the the hole with my harmonica. It's just like plugging a bathtub. Then I'll jump down, grab some tape, climb back up, and fix the hole. I'll still be a hero. Dad will be amazed. On the count of three. Here we go...one...two...three!

YES! It worked! My harmonica is sticking out the side of the sack like a small tree branch. I

quickly reverse my way back down the sugar canyon walls. I can't wait to tell Dad I finally fixed something. He'll remember this moment forever. As soon as my feet hit the ground, I...

THWACK!

Grandma and her cane are standing at the edge of the sugary forest.

"Boy, come here."

Sugar is pouring out of the holes of my harmonica. I look up.

"Boy, you better look at me," Grandma warns.

"Grandma, I can't..."

"You can't *what*?" Grandma asks. "Boy, what you lookin' at up there?"

I can feel sugar hitting the top of my head.

"Boy, is your harmonica in that bag of sugar?" Grandma points her cane at the bag just as the word *CANE* slowly rips apart.

Both of our mouths open wide. A sugar storm is approaching. And fast.

This. Is. Not. Good.

A Sticky Situation

Okay, here's the good news: Fifty pounds of sugar pouring on your head will *not* kill you. Now, the bad news: I think Grandma *might* kill me. A giant pool of sugar covers my feet and ankles. My hair looks like it was caught in a sugar snowstorm. Grandma's face is frozen. Her eyes are locked on me.

"Junior!" Grandma yells for my dad.

The door flies open. Dad stops in his tracks. He stands next to Grandma. He stares at my sugar Afro. He looks down at the pool of sugar around my ankles. Both of them have the same serious look on their faces. The silence is killing my ears. How can I can make them understand? This really wasn't my fault. Why won't they say something, grab a switch, do *anything*? Get it over with, already. I can see sugar falling from my hair as I hang my head. Then I hear something super strange.

"Ahahahaa!!" They both are *laughing*. What the heck is happening? Who *are* these people? What have they done with my dad and grandma?

"Junior, he looks just like you did. Took me a week to get all that sugar out of your hair."

I've never seen Grandma laugh this hard. Actually, I've *never* seen Grandma laugh. I am SO confused. What are they talking about? Maybe I *have* died and this is some sugar heaven dream.

Dad tells Grandma, "That was the only time Aunt Della ever yelled at me."

"You should be glad that's all she did. I shoulda taken a switch to your Black butt." Grandma sounds like her old self now.

I can't take it anymore. "What are you talking about!" I shout.

"Don't you raise your voice at me, boy." As soon

as Grandma lifts her cane, Dad pushes it back to the ground. Then he actually answers my question for once.

"It was my first winter in New York. Mama just arrived at Aunt Della's. I was so excited about seeing snow, but it wasn't coming. A week before Christmas and no snow."

Grandma finishes the story for Dad. "That boy wanted snow so badly he made a sugar snowstorm on Della's sofa bed. And the look on Melvin's face," Grandma says. This snaps Dad out of his sugar snowstorm memory.

"Mama, shush. I'm not talking about him." Dad sounds really mad at Grandma. Kinda how I sounded when he scratched my harmonica.

"Junior, gimme that note of yours," Grandma orders Dad.

"What note?"

"The one I wrote for you and Ellis. That boy was smart enough to keep his. Where's yours?"

Dad digs into his left pocket. He pulls out some cash and change, a couple of toothpicks, and a wrinkled paper. Dad opens it up for Grandma and hands it to her.

"I don't have time for this, Mama," he grumbles.

"You don't want to listen, you don't want to talk. This foolishness is going on too long now." She looks at the wrinkled note and reveals the meaning of the second mysterious acronym. Grandma thumps her cane on the floor with every word.

"Listening. Is. Tougher. Than. Talking."

Dad exits, slamming the storage room door just as Grandma says "Talking." I *never* would have guessed that fifty pounds of spilled sugar would end up with my dad being mad at my grandma instead of me. This has to be my luckiest break ever—even luckier than wiggling out of that spitball stunt with Mrs. Cook. Still, I can't help wondering...

"Grandma, who's Melvin?" I ask.

Grandma looks at me then says almost to herself, "Melvin and Junior...You and your daddy... You all have some forgivin' to do. You also need to shut your mouths and listen up. You might learn something from one another." Grandma adjusts her purse on her arm. "Go on and get you a broom and a dustpan. I want this mess gone when I come back."

What just happened? Who is Melvin? And... WHERE IS MY HARMONICA? I dive down and dig my hands underneath the pool of sugar. Got it. It tastes sweet when I put it in my mouth. I give all ten holes a blow. A small fountain of sugar sprays from each one, followed by a familiar musical note. That's a relief. I give it a good shake before sticking it in my pocket.

Now the really hard part.

I grab the small plastic fist on top of my head and pull out the comb. I can hear Mom's voice telling me it's time to pick my nappy Afro, which is just another way of saying, "It's time to comb your tangled hair." Picking a nappy Afro hurts.

Actually, my hair isn't too nappy, but it definitely has a lot of sugar in it. The best way to get rid of it is to pick it out. I push the metal teeth of the pick into my hair close to my scalp. Then I pull it up toward the top of my hair. As the pick is released from my Afro, a giant spray of sugar flies through the air. I keep picking. I'm creating my own sugar snowstorm—kinda like Dad at Aunt Della's.

"Boy, you break another bag of sugar?" Grandma asks as she returns. She changes her tone when she sees my hair. "Look at your 'fro!" she says proudly. "'Bout time you started taking care of your own hair. It looks good. You finally picked it out real good."

"Really?" I ask. "I'll be right back." I shake the sugar from my shoes and run to the bathroom.

Looking at myself through the stickers on the mirror, I can't believe what I see. I have a 'fro. A real 'fro! It looks like Wishbone's. I mean, it's not as big, but it's definitely bigger than it *used* to be. The

GROOVY sticker on the mirror looks like it's sitting right on top of my head. Better yet, my new 'fro makes me look taller. I've gotta show Dad. I find him in the front of the store staring out at Sunset.

"Dad, do you have any leftovers from American Dashiki?"

Dad looks at me, slowly tilting his head from side to side—kinda like Alex's dog when I play a really high harmonica note.

"You mean like Wishbone's?" he asks slowly.

"Shorter," I reply. "His is too long. He looks like he's wearing a dress."

"Yep. I hear that," Dad agrees. "Let me see what I can find. I like your Afro, Little Man. It makes you look taller."

"If I look taller, why are you still calling me Little Man?"

Dad starts to walk away. He's always walking away. Not this time.

"Remember what Grandma said? Listening is tougher than talking."

Dad stops but doesn't turn around. He keeps walking away toward the kitchen. I don't care if he gets mad or doesn't answer. I've got one more question for him.

"Dad? Who's Melvin?"

That one makes Dad turn around. His hand goes to his beard. He's scratching it again. I can hear the cars whizzing back and forth on Sunset Boulevard. Another police siren hurts my ears. Still, the silence in this store is deafening. Dad looks unsure if he wants to answer me. His mouth opens anyway.

"Melvin is my brother, Little Man."

My mouth drops wide open. "Your *brother*? You mean I have an *uncle*? An uncle I've never met? How come you never told me?"

"It's complicated."

"What's complicated about having an uncle?" I ask.

"Lots of things are complicated when you grow up, Little Man."

"I'M NOT A LITTLE MAN!"

I don't care that I'm not supposed to yell at my parents. This is crazy. How come Dad never told me this? How can you just forget that you have a brother? And Grandma never said anything, either. Did she forget she had another son?

Dad takes a deep breath. He's not going to say anything. I know it. Listening *and* talking are both tough for him. I stare down at the ground and do my best to not mumble.

"I want to call Mom." I know *she'll* listen.

A Long-Distance Call

Back at the Divorced Dads Bungalow, I finish our take-out Chinese food and get ready to call Mom. Dad's in his room. He hasn't said anything since I yelled at him. I keep waiting for my punishment. Even though the door is closed, I don't want him hearing my conversation. Thankfully, his telephone has an extra-long cord. I slide it under the front door and close it behind me. Then I sit down on the front stoop and dial the phone number Mom left for me. She wrote it down on a heart-shaped notepad. One ring…two rings…

"Hello?"

Hearing Mom's soft voice instantly relaxes me. I feel all of my anger and sadness race into the phone.

"Hi, Mom. It's Ellis. Can you come home now?"

I know she can't, but I had to say it. Mom asks if everything is okay. It's far from okay. I tell her about Dad's brother. There's a pause on the other end of the phone. I bet she's as surprised as me. I'm sure Mom will have *lots* to say about this. She loves to bad-mouth Dad. I can hear Mom take a breath. I know she'll make me feel better.

"Honey, I know about Melvin."

Huh? She knows?!? So everyone knows I've had an uncle except me?

Mom continues. "It's complicated, baby. So many things are complicated when you become a grown-up. Your dad has his reasons."

No way! Is she really telling me the exact same

thing Dad said? "Mom, why are you sticking up for him?"

"Just because your dad and I are divorced does not mean we disagree on *everything*. Life is complicated, Ellis."

"What's so complicated about telling me I have an uncle? I thought I could trust you, Mom."

"You *can* trust me." Mom pauses on the other end of the line. Then she says, "Parents don't always get it right, Ellis. There's some things we're still trying to figure out, too." She pauses again before she asks, "May I speak with your father?"

"Sure. Enjoy your 'me time,'" I say sarcastically. I don't even care if it's rude.

I pull the cord back inside, knock on Dad's bedroom door, and hand him the phone. Then I go back to the front stoop and sit down. As soon as my butt hits the ground, I hear a voice.

"Wow. S-sorry about your uncle."

It's the kid from Tiny Naylor's the other night. The one whose Divorced Dad lives in the bungalow across the sad garden. I didn't even notice him when I was on the phone. He obviously noticed *me*.

He walks across the sad garden and sits next to me before extending his hand.

"Jordan Sharpp with two *P-P-P*'s. Us divorced kids need to st-st-st-stick together."

"I'm Ellis," I say, shaking Jordan's hand. "I don't mean to be rude, but are you okay?"

Jordan looks almost relieved at my question. He smiles. "I'm fine. I have a sss-stutter. My words get st-st-stuck sometimes. Thanks for letting me fi-fi-fi-finish my s-s-sentence. Not everyone d-d-d-does th-at."

"No problem. Sometimes I mumble." Oh man, that was a stupid thing to say. But I guess I can work harder at speaking clearly.

The front door opens behind us. Dad steps out.

"Your mom wants to speak with you again." He gives Jordan a glance before handing me the telephone and stepping back inside. I press the phone to my ear. I'd rather keep talking to Jordan.

Mom speaks to me like I'm a baby. She acts all sweet as if nothing ever happened. "Your dad says you've been such a big help. It sounds like all you need to do is fix up that store and get yourselves some customers. How exciting."

"I guess," I say flatly. Exciting? Mom has never called any of Dad's ideas *exciting*. Although it's nice to hear her say something kind about him for once. "You're going to be here for my birthday, right?"

"I wouldn't miss it. I've got August fourth on my calendar. But first, Dad's counting on you," she says. "Do your best, Ellis. I'm sure your dad will tell you about his brother. And I'll do my best to make sure he does. Be patient. He just needs some time."

I'm not sure I believe that. But I'm glad she'll be here for my birthday. "Okay."

"I'll call you soon, baby. You're my little man. I love you."

"Bye, Mom." I hang up and turn to see Jordan. He's still here.

"You're so lucky your mom and dad st-st-still talk. M-m-my parents won't even ssss-ay each other's na-na-na-names." Jordan gets up. "Well, I hhhh-ave to get to b-b-bed."

"Hold on a second." I quickly run inside and return with a brown bag. "They're chocolate chip cookies. My dad sells them. Or he's about to sell them. Take 'em."

Jordan takes the bag and opens it. I can practically see the sugary scent curling around his nose. "Mmmm. They sm-sm-smell great. Th-th—"

"You're welcome. Us divorced kids gotta stick together." Suddenly, I realize my mistake. "Oops. I'm sorry. I didn't let you say thanks."

"It's okay. You're learning. S-s-ssssee you soon, Ellis. I'm hhhh-here with my dad every other week."

"Maybe you can come visit my dad's store when it opens. And meet my best friend, Alex. His parents aren't divorced like ours, but he's cool."

"S-s-sounds great. Th-th-th..." Jordan is getting stuck, but I just listen. I'm going to let him finish no matter how tough it is for me. After a few more stutters, he finally says, "Thanks, Ellis," then crosses the sad garden back to his divorced dad's bungalow. I should sleep, too. I'm kind of tired. And I kinda want this day to be over.

Dad's waiting for me inside wearing a stern face. He tosses me a paper bag. It's definitely not cookies. This bag is bigger. I open it. It's the dashiki I asked Dad to get me. It looks a little big, but I think I can wear it. I run to the bathroom faster than when I have to pee.

Closing the bathroom door behind me, I tear open the bag. The dashiki is blinding white. It looks like something a king would wear. A burst of colorful patterns falls down each side of the V-neck collar. They all meet at a point right in the middle. I unzip my terry-cloth shirt and quickly replace it with the dashiki. My Afro pops through the V-neck. I squeeze my eyes shut and turn on my imagination. I can see myself towering over the other kids at school. I'm not cute. I don't look like anyone's little brother. I'm a *man*. I'm a strong Black man. I open my eyes. I am…still a kid. But I look like somebody. I look like I *am* somebody.

Gazing at my reflection, I pretend I'm talking to my radio audience. "This is Ellis Johnson. Keeping. It. Real. *Always*."

I emerge from the bathroom in all of my regal dashiki glory and stand in front of Dad. His eyes

move down the river of colors around my V-neck before moving back up again. Finally, he fixes on my eyes.

"Well, look at you, Little..." Dad pauses then starts again. "Well, look at you. You are a fine young man. I'm glad I kept those dashikis in my closet." Dad's voice feels like a hug. His eyes feel like a kiss. It's funny how small things can sometimes feel really big—*so* big that they erase almost all of the bad things. A day that starts one way can end completely different.

Stepping Out Alone
on Sunset

GRAND
OPENING IN
_____ 4 ~~6~~ ~~5~~ WEEKS

The store is starting to get fixed up. It actually *looks* like a store now. An *empty* store, but still a store. The orange carpet has been replaced with a shiny wood-tiled floor. Each square tile is almost the same color as milk chocolate with a swirly wood-grain pattern.

It's like walking on a frozen chocolate lake. Right now, Dad's taking a break from the cookie dough. He's looking at a small pile of envelopes stacked on the metal table. He has his checkbook open. I've seen this before.

Back when Mom and Dad were together, they would keep a big stack of envelopes on the kitchen table. They were bills—all of the money they owed other people for rent, electricity, stuff like that. It's like the bills were a member of the family. They had their own seat at the kitchen table. The bills were always there: for breakfast, lunch, and dinner. Mom and Dad talked about the bills at every meal. Then, once a month, Dad would pull out his checkbook at the kitchen table. He would decide which ones to pay. He never paid all of them—like that time he didn't pay the electric bill. This would start Mom yelling at Dad about his crazy business ideas. "We could pay *all* these bills if you'd stop wasting our money on your stupid ideas," she'd say. Dad always responded with the same three questions. "You think my ideas are stupid? One of these ideas is gonna hit. Big. What ideas do *you* have? How about you go get yourself a job instead of giving me grief?"

Finally, Dad would bolt up from the kitchen table. "I don't want to talk about the bills." That's Dad. Never wants to talk about it. Not the bills, not Uncle Melvin, not the Rat Trap. No matter how many times or ways I ask. Nothing. Sometimes, when Dad was home, it was like he wasn't there at all.

Dad rearranges the bills next to the cookie dough like puzzle pieces. He's mumbling under his breath about which ones he can pay today and which ones can wait until later. The bills from Hollywood Bakery Supply and DMC Kitchen Repair are placed in the "later" pile. There are a few others I can't see.

"This one's gotta get paid right away so we don't get the power turned off," Dad announces, holding a bill from the Department of Water and Power. He grumbles with every number he writes before tearing out the check and stuffing it into the envelope. He licks it shut with one swipe of his tongue. "Ow!" Dad throws the envelope down. "Cut my tongue on the envelope. These damn bills." Dad hands me the envelope. "I need you to mail this for us. I'm pretty sure there's a mailbox down the street." He doesn't make a move to get up.

"Are you sure it's okay for me to walk down Sunset alone? You're not gonna watch me this time?"

"You'll be fine," Dad assures me. "No one's gonna mess with anyone wearing such a fine 'fro and dashiki. You just come right back. No detours. No distractions."

I accept my mission. I also grab a bag of cookies from the counter. Maybe I can get a few customers along the way.

It's hot outside—like inside-an-oven hot. I look for the mailbox. All I see are palm trees dotting the edge of the sidewalk. They stretch up to the sky. My eyes have a hard time seeing to the end of the block. A mailbox *has* to be down there somewhere. Dad wouldn't ask me if he wasn't sure about it. Here I go. My first walk down Sunset Boulevard on my own. I check my pick and wipe the sweat from my forehead. I look around carefully. Mom always says to check your surroundings. I kneel down to tie my shoe, but a clanking sound sends me back upright. I turn around quickly. There's a man behind me. He's pushing a shopping cart. Oh no! Is this the drunk guy who came in the store?

"Got any change, kid?" he asks. His eyes are worn but friendly. This is definitely not the drunk guy who came into the store. But he *is* very dirty like the drunk guy. I pause for a second. It looks like everything he owns is stuffed inside of his shopping cart. He's dressed for a snowstorm, not a summer day—heavy wool coat and a knit hat. His nails are dirty and longer than my mom's. He holds out a paper cup in his hand. I'm not sure what to do. I've never spoken to a homeless person before.

"No, I don't," I reply. "But here you go." I reach into my brown paper bag and place three cookies into his cup. "They're really good."

The man holds the cup to his nose. "Mmmm, they *smell* good." He rattles the cookies in his cup. Then pushes his cart into Sunset Boulevard, crossing traffic to the other side. Once he's in the shade, I see him take off his wool coat. He reaches his hand inside his cup and takes a bite of a cookie. He yells across the street, "These cookies *are* good! Crunchy! Thanks, kid!"

"You're welcome!" I shout over the cars.

Now onward to the mailbox—and to find some customers. I take two more steps before an arm blocks me. It's attached to a skinny hippie sitting on a bus bench next to a surfboard. I can see myself in his mirrored sunglasses.

"Duuude! Did you just give that homeless guy some cookies?" the surfer asks. I nod. "You got any more? I've got a long bus ride to the beach."

I open my bag. The hippie surfer takes a few cookies and immediately pops one in his mouth. "Whoa!" he says, grabbing his head. "This cookie is blowing my mind."

"It is?" I say. "Is that good?"

"Totally, dude!" the surfer confirms. "This is a magic cookie! You're a cookie magician!" I tell him about the store. He leans over the back of the bus bench, puts his nose right against mine, and whispers, "Your dad is a magician, dude. He's making cookie magic. And *you* are bringing his cookies to the people. That's beautiful, dude. Right on."

The RTD city bus arrives. The doors open. The hippie steps on with his surfboard. Just before the bus doors close, he shouts out, "Spread the cookie love, dude! I'll see you at your magic cookie store." The surfer flashes me a peace sign through the bus window as he vanishes into the traffic. I just got my second customer.

Now, onward to the mailbox. I walk past a couple FOR RENT signs before I am stopped *again*. This time, two mothers pushing baby strollers stand in front of me. They're both chewing gum. Their lips are glossy and pink like cotton candy. One of the mothers blows a big pink bubble. As it pops, she asks, "You got any more of those magic cookies, chico?"

I open my paper bag one more time. The Bubblegum Moms reach inside. They each take the gum from their mouths and stick it on their baby stroller handles.

"They're so small and cute," says one of the moms holding her cookie. The Bubblegum Moms each pop a cookie in their mouth—careful to avoid their lip gloss. Then they chew like chipmunks. And chew. And chew. They're chewing *way* too much. This cookie doesn't take that long to chew.

"I don't know if it's magic, but that's a good cookie," Bubblegum Mom One says. "And you're so handsome in that colorful shirt."

"It's a dashiki," I correct her.

"Well, whatever it is, you look handsome in it,"

Bubblegum Mom Two says, smiling. "Where can we get some more of these?"

I point down the block behind me. "My dad and I are opening a cookie store just down there. It'll be open in four weeks."

"You got yourself two customers," the Bubblegum Moms promise. They stick their gum back in their mouths and walk away down Sunset Boulevard. "Gracias, chico," they say.

Jordan, the hippie surfer, the Bubblegum Moms... I've already found four customers, and we haven't gotten to that part of the checklist yet. I continue my mailbox search with only a few cookies left. My hunt takes me to the edge of Sunset and the doorsteps of KIRA Radio. I bet Wishbone would like some cookies. Dad said no detours or distractions, but this is *technically* on the way to the mailbox. Plus, I've got to get some answers. I need Wishbone to tell me about the Rat Trap since Dad never will. Maybe he knows something about Melvin, too. This is the *opposite* of a distraction. It's a search for clues. Before I can talk myself out of it, my feet carry me up the stairs.

Operation Rat Trap

Music is blasting inside of KIRA just like before. The woman at the front desk wearing braids answers the phones.

"Excuse me," I say. "I'm here to see…"

The woman in braids cuts me off with a big smile. "Hey, honey. You're Wishbone's friend. I remember you from when the lights went out. And look at you in your dashiki. You're looking *fine*. Ready for business." She leans over the desk. "Come here, sweetie. You got something caught in your Afro there." I can smell her perfume as she pulls a yellow thread from my hair. My heart beats in my throat a little bit. She hands me the thread. "It must've come loose from your dashiki. You want that hair looking sharp."

I gulp, pushing my heart back down into my chest. She's pretty. Her skin is like midnight. I manage to say, "I brought Wishbone some cookies. Would you like one?" I open the bag. She reaches in and holds one cookie lightly between her thumb and index finger. I try to sound like a cookie scholar like Dad. "That's a perfect one. Just the right amount of chips. And check out that pecan poking through. THIS is a good cookie!"

The woman in braids giggles. "Well, you sure know your cookies. I'm gonna keep it right here on my desk and eat it after my lunch break. Maybe I can find some milk to go with it. Thank you, honey."

"We open in four weeks. Sunset Cookies. Don't forget."

"I'll be there," she says. *Yes!* I just found my fifth customer. She asks if I remember how to find Wishbone. I nod and walk down the hall to his DJ booth. Her perfume stays in my nose.

I arrive at the mothership. It sounds like a Sunday church choir is singing inside. I pull open the heavy door. Wishbone is drowning in the funk. He's waving his hands over his head. A shiny record spins on his turntable. Hand clapping and voices fill the mothership. The Sunday church choir sings through the speakers:

We've got to come together
Come together as one family
We've got to come together
Raise our voices in true harmony

Wishbone catches me out of the corner of his eye. He turns around with his hands still up in the air. Then he leans backward. His body arches like a giant, stretched-out letter *C*.

"Woooo!" Wishbone howls. "Look at Big Brother! *Soul* brother number *one!*" Wishbone lowers his arms and stands straight. He examines my new look. "The beautiful Afro, like a lion's mane. The dashiki. Lookin' like a young Zulu warrior." Then he howls again, "Woooo! Big Brother has done *found* the Promised Land!" He straightens the pick in the top of my Afro, polishing the plastic fist with his thumb. I'm glad he likes my new look, but I need to stay focused. I'm here on a mission. This is Operation Rat Trap.

The last notes of the song fade. The hand clapping and singing are replaced by the thumping of the turntable needle hitting the end of the record. It sounds like a car driving with a flat tire. Wishbone snaps out of his trance and rushes back to his microphone. He lifts the needle off the turntable and flips a switch. He then preaches to his radio audience. His voice sounds like velvet.

"My apologies, brothers and sisters. The groove swept me away. You just heard a brand-new song from California's own The Rev & The Brotherhood. It's called '(We've Got to) Come Together.' And that is the truth. This is DJ Wishbone, Keeping. It. Real. *Always*. KIRA. And now, a word from our sponsors."

Wishbone flips the switch again, pushes his

microphone away, and spins around. He points at the paper bag in my hand. "Please tell me you got your pops' cookies in there."

I almost forgot about the cookies. I hand him the bag. Wishbone opens it, shoves his nose inside, and sucks all of the air out the bag. Soon, he emerges with his blinding smile. "Sweet chocolate salvation. Your pops did it this time. This is the real deal."

"Everyone really likes them," I agree.

Wishbone swirls his hand in the bag like he's stirring soup. He then flings one cookie after another into his mouth, licking his lips after each one. Cookie crumbs fall past his gold chain and disappear into his dashiki. Wishbone holds the last cookie in his hand and spins around to the microphone. With another flip of the switch, he turns on his velvety radio voice. Cookie crumbs fly from his mouth into his microphone.

"Brothers and sisters! I have the distinct pleasure of welcoming Soul Brother Number One, Ellis Johnson, into the KIRA studio. Big Brother has given me my first taste of a sweet new sensation. THIS is a chocolate chip cookie you *wish* your mama made. And it's coming right here to Hollywood, California, in…" Wishbone covers the microphone and whispers to me, "When's your pops opening?"

"Four weeks," I whisper back.

"Coming to Hollywood in *four weeks!*" Wishbone tells his radio audience. "And it's called…" Wishbone covers the microphone again. "What's the name of this joint?"

"Sunset Cookies."

"Sunset Cookies! Do not miss this, brothers and sisters. Now, can I get an amen for the funk?!" Wishbone flips the switch and drops the needle on another record. He invites me to sit down on the chair next to him. I pull the Department of Water and Power bill from my back pocket and lay it on the desk so I don't wrinkle it.

Wishbone sucks the crumbs from his teeth while he speaks. "Your pops really did it this time, Big Brother. Those are chocolate chip cookies for the *soul.*" He doesn't seem to be speaking to me. It's more like he's speaking to Dad. I look at the posters around the mothership. Now that I have my new look, I feel like I could be in any of these bands. Then something catches my eye. It's an old photo stuck on the wall right next to the door of the mothership. I didn't see it last time. It's half-buried under a bunch of stickers, buttons, and postcards. This section of wall looks a lot like the dashboard of Dad's Rambler.

The man in the photo looks kind of like Wishbone, only his hair is shorter. And he's wearing a dark suit instead of a dashiki. A skinny tie is around his neck instead of a gold chain. He has the same big smile, though.

"Is that you, Wishbone?"

Wishbone looks up and flashes his blinding smile. "No, Big Brother, that is me before I *found* me. You know what I'm saying?"

Nope. I have *no* idea what he's saying. I realize that I basically *never* know what Wishbone is saying. He cues another album on his turntable. I study the photo. Wishbone is standing in front of a building with a crowd of people. They all look like they're celebrating. Everyone is dressed fancy. It looks like another lifetime. I can't stop staring at it.

"Wishbone, where is this?" I ask.

"The Rat Trap, Big Brother."

No way. The Rat Trap sure was a fancy place. I've got so many questions.

"Wishbone, what was the Rat Trap?"

"Shhh...no time, Big Brother. I gotta read the news on the air in one minute."

Wishbone focuses on his papers as he gets ready to read the news on his microphone. It doesn't look like he's going to tell me anything else right now. My eyes drift up to the clock above the photo on the wall. Oh no! I completely lost track of time! Dad told me to come right back. I bet if I showed this photo to Dad, he would actually tell me about the Rat Trap. I could probably take it, show it to Dad, and put it back on the wall without Wishbone even knowing it was gone. It's not stealing if I bring it back. Right…?

Sometimes you gotta take a chance. There are so many things I don't know. I don't know why my parents divorced. I basically don't know *anything* about my dad before he was my dad. Can't a kid just get a few answers about his own family? This photo feels like a clue. There's just something about it.

I'm making a final decision. Operation Rat Trap now moves into top secret mode. As Wishbone adjusts his headphones, I announce, "I gotta get back to the store. Dad's expecting me."

"Catch you on the flip, Big Brother." Wishbone waves the Department of Water and Power bill in his hand. "Don't worry. I'll mail your envelope. I got you."

Wishbone turns away to read the news. I quickly slip the photo in my back pocket. I'll return it before he ever knows it was gone. I open the door to the mothership and step out.

The Last Ingredient

I run back to the store. Things are changing fast. In the short time I've been gone, the front looks even more different. It sure doesn't feel like the Sunset Strip in here anymore. It looks...cozy. Inside, there are four square tables made of blond wood. Each table has a brass metal design cut into the center that looks like a sun. Four tall wooden chairs with comfy cushions surround each table. The big wooden counter cuts across the back of the room. It looks like one of those big wooden bars you see in old-timey Western movies. In fact, the entire store kind of looks like a Western saloon—a cookie saloon.

Dad hands out cookies to four moving men who look like bodybuilders. They are packing up their equipment. The movers gobble up the cookies instantly. Their faces light up like Christmas morning.

"Man, those are good," says one beefy mover in a gray jumpsuit. "I haven't had a chocolate chip cookie since I was a kid. I'm definitely coming back for more of these."

Dad smiles, wiping his hands on his apron. "We'll be waiting for you. Four weeks. Tell your friends."

The beefy mover is sold. "I'll *definitely* see you in four weeks. I'm gonna tell my wife."

The moving men file out of the store. Their moving truck rumbles away as Dad admires the wood floor and furniture. Now I see what he means about "a vibe."

I've gotta admit it. "It looks really great in here, Dad. It almost feels like someone's home."

"It *is* someone's home, my man. Ours," Dad

says, smiling. I can tell he's proud. I am, too. "I'd say this store is just about fixed up."

I wonder if this is the right time to pull the Rat Trap photo from my pocket and show it to Dad. He's in such a good mood. I don't know if the photo will mess that up. But...it *is* better to start a conversation while he's in a good mood. That's it. I'm doing it. Slowly, I reach my hand into my back pocket. In my head, I practice what I'm going to say to Dad. I've gotta make sure I don't mumble. Just chill, Ellis. I take a step toward Dad when he spins around and motions me to the kitchen.

"Come on. I need you back here with me," he says.

Ugh. This is gonna have to wait.

Another giant mound of chocolate chip cookie dough sits on the metal table. Some batter is still stuck inside the giant mixing bowl. Dad tosses me an apron across the table. A large silver baking sheet sits between us.

Dad explains, "This is our last batch of dough

with the chocolate chips we bought, so let's hope it's a winner. I don't know what's taking the Rock and Roll Ralphs so long to get more chips. Anyway, I already put one tray in the oven. Let's get some more in there. I want to hand them out to folks. The more people taste our cookies, the more people will show up on opening day."

We each put some flour on our hands. Dad flicks some at me.

"Hey, careful of my hair," I scold him kiddingly before splashing him with some flour of my own. We give each other a smirk from across the table. Now the cookie-dropping race begins. I pinch off some dough from the mound and move into overdrive. Before I know it, I've dropped five rows of cookie dough. I look across the tray. Dad's only dropped three rows. Yes! I dunk my leftover dough on the table, spin around, and hold up my hands. No dough on them. They're totally clean.

"I did it! I finally beat you." I shake an invisible Hula-Hoop around my waist and sing that Funkadelic song "Can You Get to That."

"Well, look at you," Dad says, admiring my

rows of cookie dough. "Your dropping game is getting strong. It must be that dashiki." Then he opens the oven door and pulls out a tray of freshly baked cookies. Man, they smell good. Dad lays the tray on the metal table. We both lean over and take a deep whiff.

"Ahhh..." We both exhale at the same time. Dad carefully lifts a hot cookie from the tray and hands it to me. We blow on them together. And just as we take a bite...

THWACK!

Grandma and her cane. I will *never* get used to it. She grabs a cookie from the hot baking sheet.

"Careful, Mama," Dad says.

Grandma brushes him aside. "Boy, I can handle a hot cookie. I've been handling hot cookies since you were a hot potato in the oven." She quickly pops it in her mouth. "Oooo! Now *this* is a good batch. Junior, I think you got it now." Grandma licks the melted chocolate from her fingers. She reaches for another one but stops when we hear a car honk in the back of the store. I poke my head through the door. Alex and his dad are getting out of their car. Mr. Reedy has a rolled-up piece of paper under his arm.

"Ooh, this must be the mysterious housewarming gift," Dad says. "I can't wait to see this, Ken."

"Well, I didn't account for your mother's *greenhouse* when I made my sketch." Mr. Reedy nods toward the little glass building Dad set up to keep all of her plants and gardening stuff.

A sketch? A sketch is kind of a strange gift for a cookie store.

Mr. Reedy continues. "It looks beautiful tucked in the corner of the parking lot. I didn't think you could fit so many plants inside of a tiny greenhouse." He wipes some flour off the table, then slowly unfurls the paper like it's a treasure map. Dad places a bag of hot cookies on one corner of the paper, and I lay my harmonica on the opposite corner. Alex pulls a couple of cookies from the bag and lays them on the last two corners. The paper actually *does* look like a treasure map. It's a bird's-eye view of the cookie store parking lot. But *this* parking lot is filled with crazy patterns and colors flowing into one another. They all meet together at the bottom corner of the page near my harmonica—right where the kitchen back door is located. Mr. Reedy has sketched a colorful cookie at the entrance of the door.

"Ken, this is marvelous!" Dad exclaims.

Dad opens the paper bag and pulls out two fresh-baked cookies. Mr. Reedy takes one. They hold them together like they're making a toast.

Mr. Reedy speaks as he chews.

"Don't talk with cookies in your mouth, Mr. Reedy," I tell him. "It's rude."

Mr. Reedy swallows then smiles. "Thanks for the reminder, Ellis." Then he turns to Dad and says, "I'm glad you like it." Mr. Reedy puts his trembling hand on my shoulder. "It looks a bit like your dashiki."

I stretch my dashiki and look down at the V-neck collar. He's right. The pattern around the collar is close to Mr. Reedy's drawing. It's the same vibe.

Grandma stares at Mr. Reedy's sketch. The colors grab her attention. "This here reminds me of Aaron Douglas. He made some big ol' murals in Harlem where Della lived."

"We're going to paint the parking lot like this?" I ask.

Dad looks at Mr. Reedy for an answer.

"We sure are," Mr. Reedy confirms. "As soon as your customers park and open their car doors, they'll step into something magical."

"That's kinda what the surfer said," I remember.

"Surfer?" Dad asks.

"The surfer on the bus bench," I explain. "I gave

him some cookies on the way to the mailbox. He said they were magic. I was getting us customers. Checking off the last thing on our list."

I can tell Dad is a little worried about me talking to strangers. He raises one eyebrow and crosses his arms. I let him know that I was really careful about checking my surroundings. His face begins to soften. He asks Mr. Reedy a question.

"What do you think about these fellas going to the Rock and Roll Ralphs to see if they finally have our chocolate chips?"

Mr. Reedy looks at Alex and me warily before nodding his approval. "I think they're big enough to handle Sunset Boulevard on their own. You just remember to keep your eyes out for characters."

Dad pulls a wad of money from his pocket and counts it carefully. "Okay, boys. Bring back as many as you can carry. Alex, make sure he keeps the chocolate chips *in* the bags this time. It's the last of the ingredients we need." He hands me the bag of cookies. "And since you're so good at sharing them, give these to our cashier friend."

I take the bag of cookies and the money. Mission accepted. This is a big deal. We will NOT mess this up. Alex and I walk out the front door onto Sunset. This must be what adulthood feels like. I can hear Dad's voice above the car traffic through the glass door.

"You come right back. No detours. No distractions."

The Chocolate Chip Hat Trick

The traffic light at the corner of Sunset and Formosa turns green. Alex and I start our walk toward the Rock and Roll Ralphs. We need to get there FAST. It's *so* hot out here. I don't want to sweat through my dashiki.

We quickly approach the second crosswalk. The Rock and Roll Ralphs is on the opposite corner. Above the store, a giant crane is lifting the last section of a new billboard into place.

The billboard is painted like a giant American flag—except this flag only has thirteen stars.

HAPPY BIRTHDAY, AMERICA!
1776-1976

AMERICAN BICENTENNIAL
"That all men are created equal"

They're all in a circle. I see flags EVERYWHERE lately. This has been the longest birthday ever. Why do people keep talking about something that happened so long ago? Three old-timey white men are painted in the center of the billboard. They look like soldiers but instead of holding guns, they are holding instruments. Two have a big drum hanging from each of their necks. The one on the end is playing a flute. I hold my harmonica to my mouth and move one leg forward like I'm ready for war. After blowing a battle charge with my harmonica, I check my pick. I want to make sure the plastic fist is sticking straight up. Then I point up at the billboard and ask, "Do I look like one of those guys?"

Alex looks at the billboard above. He looks at my old-timey soldier pose. "Not at all," he says.

"You don't know what you're talking about," I tell him. "Four score and seven years ago, our fathers brought forth the funk."

"I don't think that's what Abraham Lincoln said."

The doors slide open, and a wave of cold air greets us at the Rock and Roll Ralphs. The air-conditioning feels SO good. We grab the last shopping cart. A loose wheel in the front makes the whole thing move with a stutter. It's rattling and shaking across the store. Alex and I stop the cart at aisle ten. The aisle of shame. Our chocolate chips have come in. The entire shelf is full this time. I look at the wall of yellow bags stacked on top of one another. There's no way I'm making the same mistake again. I ask Alex to reach up and grab the chips at the top of the stack. He easily grabs one. No need for him to climb up the shelf. It helps to have a best friend who's tall. Alex tosses the first bag at the shopping cart.

"Reedy shoots for two points," he says. I quickly pull the shopping cart back. The bag misses and lands on the floor. Alex's blank look makes me crack up. I can't stop laughing. "Um, Ellis," he says, pointing at the floor.

"Uh-oh," I gasp. The bag broke. Chocolate chips are scattered across the floor like marbles. I push the shopping cart closer to the shelf. Then I tell Alex, "Gimme your hat."

"No way!" He refuses. "You're not gonna put chocolate chips in my favorite hat."

"C'mon, Alex," I beg. I can't let anyone see this. Not after what happened last time. "Just give me your hat."

Alex reluctantly gives me his Dodgers baseball cap. I quickly collect all of the chocolate chips inside of it. Then I hand it back to him.

"Put it on."

"What? No way."

"*C'mon*, Alex," I beg once more. "We'll pay for the bag, but we can't let anyone know we broke it. You can dump them as soon as we're outside."

I have to admit, I wouldn't want to do it, either. But sometimes you have to take one for the team.

"Why can't *you* wear it?" Alex asks.

"Because it'll mess up my 'fro, obviously. And it won't fit over my pick."

Alex understands. He reluctantly takes his Dodgers cap, leans over, and sticks his head inside. Then he slowly stands up. Perfect! No chips fell out. Now we just have to pay for everything and get out of here.

In the checkout line, Alex looks nervous. Too nervous. I can tell because he's sweating on his upper lip. I lean over and whisper, "Chill out." We push our stuttering shopping cart next to the cashier. She eyes the cart overflowing with chocolate chips.

"Hey! You're that cookie boy," she remembers. "How's that store coming along?" she asks. I hand her the bag of cookies Dad gave me.

"Great. We open in four weeks. These are from my dad. Freshly baked."

The cashier takes the bag and sets it down next to her cash register. She's too distracted by Alex to try a cookie.

"Well, *that's* unusual," the cashier says. "It's not every day you see someone with chocolate running down their face."

Oh, great. He's sweating chocolate.

"Nope, you don't see that every day," I say. *"This*  is highly unusual." I hand her the empty bag of chocolate chips. "You probably won't believe this, but we found this empty bag of chocolate chips on aisle ten." I hand her the money Dad gave me. "We'd like to pay for it along with the other bags. Not because we did anything wrong. Just because this is our supermarket. Us neighborhood businesses need to support each other. You know?"

The cashier nods. "Oh, yeah. I know."

"Speaking of which, I hope you'll come to our store when we open in..."

The cashier cuts me off. "Four weeks. I heard you."

She hands me my change then watches us push our stuttering shopping cart away. "You got a bad cart. Those are supposed be sent to the scrapyard. Go ahead and take it with you. It's hot outside. Pushing a bad cart is still easier than carrying those chips in your arms...or your hat." She winks.

Shopping Cart Drag Race

It's hot enough outside the Rock and Roll Ralphs to fry an egg—or melt a shopping cart full of chocolate chips. The cookie store is only two blocks away, but we need to move quickly or else we'll have a bunch of chocolate soup. In fact, Alex now has chocolate soup pouring down his head as he takes off his Dodgers cap.

"Ellis, you ruined my cap," Alex says.

I change the subject. "You're the one who started sweating. Let's just hurry. We'll clean your hat when we get to the store." I move to the front of the cart and tell Alex, "Okay, you push."

"Why do *I* have to push?" Alex objects.

"Because you're a faster runner," I say. "You have longer legs. Besides, I have to keep the chocolate chips from falling out. We've got this thing packed."

Once again, Alex understands. That's why we're best friends. I step up backward onto the bottom tray of the shopping cart. Facing forward, I grab the basket behind me. Alex pushes off. Our stuttering shopping cart rattles across the Rock and Roll Ralphs parking lot in between the parked cars. I can barely hang on to the front. This is going to be a rough ride. It feels like my teeth might fall out of my mouth. I need to get my balance. I turn around to face Alex—and catch a bag before it falls overboard.

"See? The chips need protection."

We wobble off the parking lot and stop at the end of the block. The traffic light reads DON'T WALK. Alex looks past me to the other side of the crosswalk. "Hey, Ellis. Remember when my dad said we should keep our eyes out for characters?"

I nod while keeping the slippery bags from sliding off the pile.

"Maybe we should go to the other side of the street."

I step down from the cart, turn around, and look to the other side of the crosswalk. A shopping cart is parked next to a large metal-wire trash basket with a sign that says KEEP HOLLYWOOD CLEAN. The man I met earlier is digging in the trash basket as if he lost something.

"Oh, he's okay," I tell Alex.

"He is?"

"Yeah, I'm positive."

The traffic light changes to WALK. Alex is still unsure if he wants to cross. He watches the man as he comes up from the trash basket. He locks eyes with me, raises his hand, and smiles.

"Hey! Cookie kid!" he shouts.

I wave back. "How you doing?" I shout.

Alex looks at me in disbelief. "You're friends with that guy?" he asks.

"I wouldn't say we're friends," I clarify. "I gave him some cookies earlier. He's nice."

Now Alex feels safe. He pushes through the crosswalk and brings us to a stop next to the man's shopping cart. Our pile of chocolate chips sits beside his pile of...stuff. It looks like the start of a drag race.

"Nice shopping cart!" he compliments us.

"Thanks," I say. "The cashier at the Rock and Roll Ralphs let us take it. It's got a bad wheel, though."

"Bad wheel? Oh, I can fix that, no problem," the man offers. "These carts are always getting bum wheels."

He gets on his hands and knees, examining the wheel. He fishes for something in his pocket. After a moment, he removes a handful of tiny silver pellets.

"These shopping cart wheels are almost exactly like skateboard wheels," he explains like an auto mechanic. "If they lose their ball bearings, they get all wobbly."

The man inserts two of his BBs near the center of the wheel. He stands up and takes the shopping cart from Alex, moving it back and forth. It's not stuttering anymore.

"I got these from a broken skateboard someone threw away," he says. "You never know when things will come in handy." The man hands the shopping cart back to Alex. "This is a good cart. Hold on to this one," he says. He pushes his own cart into the crosswalk toward the Rock and Roll Ralphs just as the traffic light flashes DON'T WALK.

"See ya, cookie kid!"

Alex wipes some melted chocolate from his face. "That's the coolest homeless guy I have ever met," he says, amazed.

I am positive that is the *only* homeless guy Alex has ever met. Now we need to get back to the store. The chocolate chips are melting fast. We have one long city block left. The sidewalk is clear as far as we can see. Our shopping cart is good as new. I take my position at the front, looking straight ahead. It's showtime.

Alex grips the handle. He stretches his right leg back like a runner starting a hundred-yard dash. We're ready. We're going to save these chips. I point forward like a ship captain at sea spotting land.

"Full steam ahead!" I roar. Alex plows our

shopping cart forward, keeping his head low. We barrel down Sunset. The ride is smooth. The hot Hollywood air whips our faces. Alex reaches one hand forward. He does his best to hold down the bags of chocolate chips. The corner of Sunset and Formosa is fast approaching. And so is another DON'T WALK sign. A steady stream of cars rounds the corner in front of us.

I yell behind me, "Stop the cart! The light is red!"

Alex tries pulling the cart to a stop, but we're moving too fast. He's not strong enough. We're going to fly into the crosswalk and get hit by these cars. I see my eleven years flash before my eyes. Is *this* how it ends? Not crushed under a mountain of chocolate chips. Not buried in an avalanche of sugar. But smashed in a shopping cart on Sunset Boulevard?

"NOT TODAY, SATAN!"

I step my feet off the bottom of the shopping cart. I push my legs forward and dig my heels into the cement sidewalk. The rubber soles of my shoes start wearing down like an eraser. My hands cling behind me to the cart.

"Pull, Alex!" I holler.

The corner is almost here. I see the cookie store on the other side of the crosswalk. The red traffic light and DON'T WALK sign stare us in the face. A motorcycle speeds past the crosswalk right in front of us. It's no use. I pull my feet back up onto the cart just as the front wheels fly over the curb. Alex jumps onto the back. Our cart sails across the intersection of Sunset and Formosa...just as the DON'T WALK sign changes to WALK.

Now in the middle of the crosswalk, we've slowed down enough for Alex to jump off the back. He pushes all of his weight down onto the handle. This sends the front of the cart into a small wheelie. The front wheels clear the next curb. Our shopping cart makes a perfect stop in front of the cookie store. Did that just happen? Alex and I look at each other in amazement.

"YES!" we yell. One palm slap, two fist bumps, then grab pinky fingers. I swear I can hear people clapping. Actually...wait...I *do* hear people clapping. It's Dad and Mr. Reedy.

"That's quite a ride you boys have there," Mr.

Reedy says. "You both are genuine Hollywood action movie heroes."

Dad holds open the front door and says, "You both can explain this once we get these chocolate chips out of the heat."

Alex and I push the shopping cart through the front door. We saved the chocolate chips—and ourselves. Now we have all the ingredients. Another item crossed off Dad's list. And on top of that, I have an idea to get us more customers.

Uncle Melvin Is...

Every store needs a delivery vehicle. This shopping cart will be ours.

"It's perfect, Alex," I begin convincing him. "We already know it's fast. We know it will fit lots of cookies. We can make deliveries up and down the Sunset Strip. It will be perfect for getting new customers, too. When people see us, they'll definitely want some cookies."

Alex isn't so convinced.

"You have to push, too. It's harder than you think."

That seems fair. "If I push, will you help make it look like a cookie cart?"

Alex thinks hard on it then nods. "Okay."

"Deal. Dad's gonna love it."

We give each other the secret handshake. Now we need to make this shopping cart look like a cookie cart. Starting with a sign. I carefully rip one of the sides from a cardboard box. Then, using my pick, I poke two holes into the cardboard. Alex grabs the string from an empty sugar sack, and we attach the cardboard to the front of the cart. It's ready. I ask Alex to get a marker from the kitchen. He pulls off the cap and hands it to me. From this day forward, this shopping cart shall be known as...

THE SUNSET COOKIE RACER

Alex and I push the racer through the kitchen and onto the parking lot. Grandma is sleeping in the corner of her greenhouse with the front door wide open. She's passed out in her folding chair. Her big floppy sun hat is pulled over her face. The soft brim of the hat floats up above her mouth with every one of her snores. Grandma can sleep through *anything.* That's good for us because this cart is rattling pretty loudly on the cracked pavement.

Alex and I take a few test runs around the parking lot. If we're going to make deliveries, we need to be prepared for anything. Alex pushes the racer as fast as he can, then jumps on the back. This cart moves a lot faster without the chips inside. It's more like a go-kart than a cookie cart. I throw myself into the empty basket like it's a race car cockpit. Alex leans hard to one side and makes one big circle around the parking lot with only one push. Run, jump, and lean. Run, jump, and lean. This is better than riding Alex's BMX bike down our street at home. The parking lot has become our racetrack. The side of the racer breezes close to Grandma's greenhouse on the last hairpin turn. A little *too* close. Alex quickly pulls the racer to a stop. I'm panting from the ride.

"Why are *you* out of breath? You said you were going to do some pushing, remember?"

"Okay, okay, I'll push. You're gonna love riding in the basket. It's so scary."

I climb out of the cart and adjust my dashiki. I also check the Rat Trap photo in my back pocket. I just realized I probably shouldn't be sitting on it.

"Uh-oh," I say, straightening a dog-eared corner.

"What's that?"

I hand Alex the photo.

"It's Wishbone before he was Wishbone."

"Huh?"

"It's complicated. Just put it in your shirt pocket. Come on, I know where I can push the cart so you're really scared."

I will admit—I'm not one hundred percent sure about this idea. But sometimes you gotta take a chance. I stand behind the racer at the top of Formosa. The cookie store sits one block below. This hill is a lot steeper than I thought. But at least it doesn't have a curve or any hairpin turns. Alex sits inside the cart, looking straight toward Sunset.

"Maybe I *should* push."

"No way. I got this. You're going to love it. It's like

riding your BMX down our hill but only better." I explain the plan. "After I push off, we'll race straight down the sidewalk. When I say 'Now,' we lean our weight to the left so we turn onto the cookie store driveway. Once we're in the parking lot, I'll jump off and pull us to a stop. What could go wrong?"

This time, Alex is not easily convinced. "Uh, let's see. What could go wrong? We miss the driveway? You can't stop the cart? We crash straight into Sunset Boulevard? This is nothing like riding our bikes down our hill at home."

"Chill out. We'll be fine."

I examine the sidewalk in front of us. There are a couple of big cracks halfway down the hill. The roots from a huge avocado tree have buckled the concrete into something like a small skateboard ramp. No problem. Here we go.

"On the count of three," I say.

"No!" Alex responds.

"One...two...THREE!"

I push the racer three steps down the hill then jump on the back. I grip the shopping cart handle super tight. The racer picks up speed fast, clattering over the sidewalk lines. Each time the wheels roll over a line, my feet nearly slip off. The rattling is loud...but not as loud as Alex screaming.

The broken concrete is getting close. The racer rolls up the ramp and takes flight. We're airborne for a few feet before our racer bangs to the ground. The parking lot driveway is coming up fast. A little too fast.

"Now!" I yell above the clanking and Alex's screaming.

We lean all of our weight to the left. This is definitely one of those times I wish I was taller—and heavier. If we don't turn into the driveway, this cookie cart will roll straight into Sunset traffic. About a hundred feet to go. I push down harder on the left side of the handle. Alex leans into the left side of the cart. Yes! We're leaning left. No! We're leaning TOO far left. The right wheels have come off the ground. We're seconds from falling over.

"Now right!" I yell.

"Now right *what*?"

"Now lean back to the right."

We shift our weight. This gets all four wheels back on the ground just as we roll onto the parking lot. But we're moving fast. AND...we're on a collision course with Grandma's greenhouse. I see her through the open door, still sleeping. I jump off the back of the racer and try to drag it to a stop. It's no use. I'm not strong enough.

"Grandma!" I yell. "Wake up!"

Nothing. The soft brim of her hat floats up above her mouth again. I can only imagine how loud her snoring sounds inside that greenhouse. It's definitely louder than the sound of this rattling cart only...*a few feet from her.* Our racer rolls through the open door of the greenhouse. Plants splatter across the inside. One of Grandma's spider plants soars into the air, hits the top of the greenhouse, and falls back down. Down...down... squarely on Grandma's head.

The Sunset Racer stops inches away from Grandma. Her floppy sun hat is covered in dirt. The spider plant sits on top of her head like a bad wig. Is she breathing? Yep. Her snore shakes the brim of her hat. Some dirt slides off the brim and onto her face. THIS wakes her. Grandma bolts up in her chair and shakes the spider plant from her head. She looks past Alex and focuses her eyes on me standing behind the racer.

It's coming. I know it is.

"BOY. COME. HERE."

Grandma is fuming. She looks around her wrecked greenhouse. I've done it this time. This is the worst one yet.

"Grandma, I'm sorry," I beg. Those might be my last words.

She reaches for her cane to stand up. I seriously wonder if I should run, but I can't leave Alex. Grandma stops when she sees the photo poking out of Alex's shirt pocket. She yanks it out. Suddenly, Grandma's not so angry anymore.

"Lord, will you look at that," she says, recognizing Wishbone's face in the photo. Then she blurts out, "Look at my baby, Melvin."

Excuse me. Did she just say *MELVIN*?

"Wishbone is Melvin?" I shout. "Wishbone is my uncle Melvin?"

I grab the photo from Grandma's hands so I can study it again. Usually, Grandma would yell at me for grabbing something without permission, but not this time. She lets me keep it, and breathes a heavy sigh.

"It's time Melvin and your daddy stopped playing these games. This family needs to come together. Eight years is too long."

I can't believe this. Uncle Wishbone. Now *that* is funky.

Where the Sun Sets

Dad storms out of the back kitchen door onto the parking lot. He looks at the wrecked greenhouse. "Dang it, Ellis, what happened *this* time?" he asks angrily.

How do I answer that question? *Why* should I answer that question? No one has answered *any* of my questions. Everyone just keeps secrets and lies. Wishbone, Grandma, Mom, Dad…they all knew he was my uncle. How can you keep that a secret for my *entire* life?! My hands are balled into fists. My lip has that shaky feeling like I'm about to cry.

"What *happened*?" I ask. "What happened is that Grandma told me that Wishbone is my uncle."

Dad looks like he saw a ghost. It's that same look he had when Wishbone first came to the store. He glances at Grandma. I can tell he's upset with her.

"Grandma didn't do anything wrong," I say before he blames her. "At least she cares enough to finally tell me the truth."

Grandma looks like she might ask me to get a switch from her greenhouse. Instead, she says softly, "Go on, boy. You tell your daddy how you feel."

Suddenly, I don't want to tell *anyone* how I feel, especially Dad, and I definitely don't want to hear his excuses. *Wishbone is my UNCLE. And no one told me.* I just want to be as far away from this stupid kitchen as I can. I run across the parking lot, race through the store, and unlock the front door. Then I take off down Sunset until I get to the bus bench. I sit down and put my face in my hands. They are soaked from the sweat on my forehead and the tears from my eyes. I'm not even sure why I'm crying. All I know is I want to go far away. I stare at the photo. Wishbone even looks a little like Dad. How did I not see this before? Alex catches up with me and sits down by my side.

"Man, I'm sorry you're having a hard time, Ellis." I look up as a RTD city bus approaches. The sign over the front windshield reads SUNSET EXPRESS TO BEACH. I stand up.

"Hey, where are you going?" asks Alex.

"I don't know. Away from here."

The bus stops and the door opens. The bus driver looks old enough to be my grandfather.

His beard is the same as Dad's but with more gray hair.

"You riding, son?" he asks.

Yes, I want to ride. I step on the bus, hiding my tears. I can feel Alex behind me on the steps.

"You should go back. I don't want you to get in trouble." Alex looks worried, but he steps back off the bus.

"Be careful, Ellis," Alex says. "I'll be here when you get back."

I dig in my pocket for some change from the Rock and Roll Ralphs. Two quarters is what I need. Found them. They drop to the bottom of the fare box. The bus driver closes the door and motions to the front row of seats over his shoulder. There's a sticker on the window behind the row of seats.

PRIORITY SEATING. PLEASE OFFER THIS SEAT TO SENIORS.

"It's okay. You sit up here by me, buddy," he offers kindly.

I squeeze next to a large woman. She holds two bags of groceries and a big purse on her lap. Her purse looks like Grandma's. This bus is very different from a school bus. The Sunset Strip looks huge through the bus window. The buildings, cars, and sky are all mixed together. I turn around and look at the people at the back of the bus. Some are sleeping with their heads against the window. Others are reading books. There is a man in the very last row. He sounds like he is arguing with himself.

"Don't pay him no attention," says the large woman next to me. "His mind ain't right. Just be glad we're sittin' up here. Not so long ago we would've been back there with him." The woman reaches into her purse, pulls out a tissue, and hands it to me. "Looks like you could use this."

The bus driver pulls over at the next bus stop and opens the door. Through the windshield I can see a familiar bright yellow one-story building on the corner. The words TOWER RECORDS are mounted on the side in big red capital letters. Our favorite store in the whole world. They have every kind of music. Alex and I have to beg our parents to drive us here so we can buy albums. Then they usually have to come inside and drag us out.

I had no idea you could get on the bus and come here.

Two men get on board. They are holding hands like they're married. Both of them wear matching super-tight shorts and tank tops. Their arms are bigger than my legs. They sit by the back door and look at a magazine together. I can see the cover. It's called *Muscle*. The bus driver closes the door and steers the bus back into traffic.

"Where you headed, buddy?" he asks.

"I dunno," I mumble.

Soon, all of the stores and buildings disappear and are replaced by mansions. They're tucked behind iron gates and surrounded by giant green lawns. Fancy sports cars are parked in some of the driveways. I've never seen houses this big. There are no characters walking on the sidewalks. No billboards. No one pushing shopping carts. The bus driver must know it's my first bus ride.

"Beverly Hills is a long way from Hollywood," he says. "A whole lotta money here."

The woman next to me digs into her grocery bag and pulls out an orange. She peels it in one piece and offers me a slice. Then she sniffs me.

"You smell like a bake shop," she says, peeling off an orange slice for me.

"It's cookies," I explain. Right now, I'm really hating the smell of cookies.

The neighborhoods keep changing. The Beverly Hills mansions are now gone. I see a hospital, a college, a giant pink hotel. The neighborhoods change so fast on Sunset. It's funny...all different types of people live next to each other on this one street, and they don't even know it. I bet the people in those Beverly Hills homes have never driven down Sunset to eat at Tiny Naylor's. I never knew Sunset stretched so far until I got on this bus.

After a few more winding turns, I see the ocean up ahead. The sun is hanging low in the sky over the water. That must be why they call this Sunset Boulevard. It runs all the way west to the Pacific Ocean where the sun sets.

The Sunset Express makes its last stop at the beach. Only three passengers are left on the bus: the large woman, the guy who's yelling at himself, and me. The bus driver opens the door. The man in the last row exits through the back, shouting at himself as he walks down the beach. The air is a lot cooler here by the ocean. I'm not sure what to do. I'm not even sure how to get back to the store—even if I wanted. And I *don't* want to go back. I look at the woman.

"Are you getting off here?" I ask.

"Nah, honey," she says. "I live near downtown. I just like coming out west and looking at the water. Relaxes my nerves. It's quiet. Reminds me to listen. Listening is tougher than talking."

"That's what my grandma says," I tell the woman.

The woman starts peeling another orange. "She sounds like a smart lady."

"I guess," I mumble. "My dad doesn't listen."

"What's your name, baby?"

"Ellis. Ellis Johnson."

"I'm Thelma, sweetheart." She offers me another orange slice. I take a bite, catching some of the juice before it lands on my dashiki. I wipe it on my pants just as I hear...

"Duuude!"

Cosmo's Surfer Society

It's the hippie surfer. He's holding his surfboard, and his flip-flops are covered in sand. A motley group of kids stands behind him. I quickly count them all in my head. There's five boys and three girls, all holding surfboards of their own. They look like high schoolers.

"Are you a teacher?" I ask the hippie surfer.

"All of us are teachers, dude. I'm just here helping my friends learn to catch the wave."

A kid with a freckled, sunburned nose shouts out, "He's a teacher."

The hippie surfer faces the group after paying his two quarters. "Alright, everyone, have your bus fare ready and remember our buddy system. We all sit next to someone."

One by one, everyone pays the fare then takes a seat near the front of the bus. Instead of sitting in one of the empty seats, the hippie surfer wedges himself into the front row, so now I'm smushed between his surfboard and Thelma.

"I have always wanted to surf," she tells the surfer. Thelma leans across me and offers him an

orange slice. He takes a bite. Juice runs down his chin.

"All are welcome in the Surfer Society."

A scrawny boy seated in the second row eyes my dashiki. "You look like a surfer."

"Me? I don't know how to surf. Seems kinda scary." I can't believe these older kids are talking to me. One of them wearing a T-shirt with the words *Hang Loose* leaves his surfboard at his seat and walks up to me.

"Dude, if you're brave enough to ride a bus by yourself, you can surf. I was *totally* scared to ride the bus alone when I was your age."

"Totally," says one of the surfer girls. "I wish my little brother would go an adventure by himself. He won't even leave his room."

Another surfer kid calls out to the hippie surfer. Her nose is sunburned, too. Her wet hair is pulled back in a ponytail.

"Hey, Cosmo, is this the cookie kid you were talking about?"

The hippie surfer is named Cosmo? That is perfect. Cosmo stands up, wipes the orange juice from his chin, and makes an announcement to his surfer class.

"This is indeed the cookie kid." Cosmo looks at me while waving his arms across the surfer group. "And these are the young men and women of Cosmo's Surfer Society. Chasing the wave every Wednesday."

"I love a good cookie," says the bus driver.

"They're *magic* cookies," Cosmo clarifies.

"A magic cookie?" Thelma lights up. "I gotta try me that."

Soon, I'm surrounded by the entire Surfer Society. One by one, they introduce themselves. I think they like me. They immediately start asking questions about the cookie store. Yesterday, I would have jumped at the chance to get Dad and me some new customers. But now, I'm not really in the mood to talk about it. I might not ever go back to that store.

"Where can I get a shirt like that?" one of them asks me. "It's off the hook."

"I can't believe your parents let you come to the beach alone. My parents wouldn't let me go anywhere alone until I was way older. What are you doing out here, anyway?"

Cosmo and his Surfer Society, the bus driver, and Thelma all look at me, waiting for an answer. At first I don't know what to say. Then I take a deep breath and tell them. Everything. I tell them about Mom and Dad's divorce, the Rat Trap, the photo, Uncle Melvin, my twelfth birthday that no one cares about, all of it. No mumbling. It feels good to tell somebody—even a bunch of strangers on a bus. When I'm done talking, they all keep staring at me. After a few seconds, Cosmo breaks the silence.

"Dude, that's a heavy story."

"Super heavy," says the scrawny boy.

"I wish I had an uncle. Both of my parents are only kids like me," says the girl with the wet ponytail.

"I'm an only kid, too," I tell her.

Thelma puts her grocery bags on the ground then turns her body toward me. She takes my hands and looks at me like my mom sometimes does.

"All I know is this. Any two grown men not talking to each other for *eight whole years* are in a lot of pain. Your daddy and uncle have broken hearts, baby. Just like yours."

"Big time, dude," says Cosmo.

The large woman lets go of my hands. "You are the one who can fix this. That daddy and uncle of yours are *begging* you to bring them together. They just don't know how."

"*You're* the magic, dude," Cosmo says.

"Cosmo's right," says the freckled, sunburned surfer.

A boy who's short like me steps forward. "The Surfer Society stands with you. Work it out with your dad. Then come surf with us someday. We could use kids like you in the Society."

These surfers are really nice. Especially for teenagers. Maybe it's the ocean air. The bus driver closes the door and starts the engine.

"Everybody take your seats," he says. He pulls the bus into a U-turn and drives it back into traffic. As he steers it back down Sunset, he says to me, "We're getting you back to that cookie store, buddy."

The Shoeshine Box

It's getting dark over Sunset Boulevard. The bus stops across the street from the cookie store. I see Dad through the window pacing back and forth. His wooden mixing spoon is in his hand. That can't be good. Is he taking a page from Grandma's book? A spoon's gonna hurt a whole lot more than a switch. The bus driver turns off the engine and opens the door. I'm still wedged in between Cosmo and Thelma. The last Surfer Society kid got off the bus a few stops ago with a high five and a "good luck." I'm going to need all of the luck I can get. I've been gone for almost four hours. I know Dad's going to be super mad.

"Alright, buddy." The bus driver looks at me. "I'll walk you across the street."

I don't move. I'm not *going* to move. I'm staying on this bus forever.

"Come on, baby," Thelma says kindly. "We're all going with you."

Cosmo grabs his surfboard and stands up. The large woman reaches into her grocery bag and hands me her last orange.

"That's right, dude," Cosmo says. "We're in this together."

I look at Cosmo, the bus driver, and Thelma. It feels like I've known them forever. Mom always says to watch out for characters, but right now, the characters are watching out for *me*.

We all step off the bus and cross the street. As we reach the front of the store, the bus driver gently nudges me up front. I take a deep breath and knock on the glass door. Dad dashes forward. I can see Cosmo, the bus driver, and Thelma behind me in the reflection of the door. They make me feel safe. Dad and I look at each other through the glass. He actually looks happy to see me. That's a relief. But he's still holding that spoon.

Dad unlocks the door, drops the spoon, and wraps me in his arms. I blow a sigh of relief and lay my head against his apron. Flour gets on my cheek. Then I look up at Dad. He's crying. Not a lot. But he's definitely crying. I see one teardrop from the corner of his eye. It's barely visible on his dark skin. It rolls off his face and lands on my forehead. I've never seen Dad cry before.

"Your grandma was right," Dad whispers in my ear. "Listening is tougher than talking. I haven't done a very good job of listening or talking. I'm sorry for that."

Dad has never said he's sorry about anything. I can feel him squeeze me harder. Wait a minute. That's not Dad. Someone is squeezing me from behind.

"Duuuude, this is so beautiful," Cosmo announces to everyone. His arms are wrapped around my dad. I'm sandwiched in between them. He pushes his face against Dad's. I can hear him whisper above me, "Your cookies are magic."

Thelma delicately pulls Cosmo away.

"Easy now, baby," she says. "This ain't your moment."

Dad looks at my friends standing behind me. "Aren't you going to introduce me?" Before I can say anything, they introduce themselves to Dad one by one.

"Cosmo Guthrie. Stoked to meet you, sir. It's an honor to step inside of this magic cookie palace."

"This must be the surfer you told me about," Dad says. I nod.

"John Moses," the bus driver says, shaking Dad's hand. "Hope your boy didn't have you too worried. We took good care of him."

"Thelma Elmore," says the large woman. Then she looks at me and says, "Aunt Thelma to you." She tells Dad, "This is a special boy you got here."

Dad looks at me and says, "He's my one and only son. That makes him *extra* special." Dad wipes his eye then disappears into the back. He returns with three brown paper bags. He hands a bag to Cosmo, John Moses, and Aunt Thelma.

"Thank you for getting my man back here safely," he says. "Cookies are on me when we open."

Cosmo, John Moses, and Aunt Thelma each give me a hug and cross Sunset back to the bus. I wave goodbye while Dad locks the door. He turns off the lights in the front.

"C'mon, my man," he says. "There's something I want to show you at home."

Dad walks into his bedroom as soon as we get to his place. He's acting serious. It feels like he still might punish me. I put Aunt Thelma's orange in the refrigerator with Dad's oranges. Actually, I should eat it. We're definitely not going to Tiny Naylor's tonight. I sit down at the small dining table and try peeling the orange in one piece like Aunt Thelma did on the bus. No luck. Dad steps out of the bedroom holding a beat-up wooden box. He sets it on a chair in between us. He eyes me peeling the orange before grabbing his own from the refrigerator.

"Here's the secret," Dad says, holding his orange.

"You start at the top by the stem. Get your thumb underneath. Peel slowly." Dad unwraps the peel around his orange. He lays it on the table in one piece. "Now you try it."

I dig my thumb into the top of my orange and slowly bulldoze under the peel. Very slowly.

"See? You did it." As we eat our oranges for dinner, Dad lifts the wooden box on the table. It's about the same size as a shoebox. The wood is worn like an old floor. There is a metal latch on one side.

A footrest sits on top of the box. It actually looks like the sole of a shoe.

"This was my shoeshine box," Dad says proudly. "The one I took with me on the train to New York." He's not looking serious anymore. I'm pretty sure I'm not getting punished tonight.

Dad opens the box like it's a treasure chest. It smells like paint fumes—probably from the old cans of shoe polish inside. The box is filled with all sorts of random stuff. There are tarnished coins, a bow tie, shoelaces, a crinkly newspaper article, and an envelope. I take the envelope out of the box. It's unsealed and stuffed with photos. Slowly, I pull them out. I can't believe what I'm seeing. This is my family story. It's been here all along—hidden in an envelope, tucked inside of an old shoeshine box, at the bottom of my dad's closet.

I spread the photos across the table like pieces of a map. I see two little boys with their arms around each other. One of them is wearing the bow tie from the box.

"Wishbone," Dad explains. "That's Melvin and me."

There's another photo of Wishbone and Dad standing outside of the Rat Trap.

I show Dad my photo of Wishbone.

"Melvin give this to you?"

"Uh...kinda."

Luckily, Dad isn't too concerned about how I got the photo. He's too busy talking. Finally.

"One of the first Black-owned music clubs in Harlem. Opened our doors March ninth, 1964. Melvin and I had *everyone* coming. Dancing, music, Black folks and white folks gettin' *down*. It was a funky joint."

He tells me story after story about the Rat Trap. It sounds like it was the coolest club ever. People in their fanciest clothes would line up around the block waiting to get inside. All sorts of bands would play live music.

My head is spinning. I pull another photo from the shoeshine box. It's Wishbone, Dad, and me in front of the Rat Trap. I'm just a baby. Dad's arms are wrapped around me.

"Your mom had a rough time giving birth to you," Dad tells me. "You may be little now, but you were a *big* baby. The Rat Trap just had its grand opening and I had to work so I brought you with me."

"Did I see any bands play?" I ask.

"Oh, yeah. Plenty. You spent the first few years of your life in that club." Dad smiles. "Muddy Waters came through once."

"Muddy Waters! Are you serious?"

Dad nods. "I'm serious. How do you think I know the words to 'Mannish Boy'?"

I dig through the shoeshine box looking for more stories. I pull out a crinkly newspaper page. It's folded in half. A small article in the corner of the page is circled with a marker. I read the headline:

NEW YORK NIGHTCLUB, RAT TRAP, CLOSED
CO-OWNER MELVIN JOHNSON ARRESTED

WHAT? Wishbone arrested? So much for having the coolest uncle. I read more of the article. Wishbone was stealing money from the Rat Trap. For nearly three years, Dad had no idea. I can't believe I wanted to have a clubhouse like his mothership. No wonder Dad didn't speak to him. Stealing from your own brother?

Dad says almost to himself, "Family is tougher than time." Then he pauses. "I think I know what Grandma means. And *you* helped me figure it out. Families make mistakes, Ellis."

"I made a mistake getting on that bus, Dad. I'm sorry."

"You made a mistake not telling me where you were going," Dad says. "That bus ride did both of us some good. Plus, you got us some new customers." Then he wrinkles his forehead and adds, "But don't you ever do that again, you hear me?" Dad splits apart the last two slices of his orange and hands one to me. "You hear me?"

"I hear you."

As we chew, Dad promises, "I'm gonna speak with your uncle. I am. I just need a little more time."

The Mayor of
Sunset Strip

GRAND
OPENING IN
~~4~~ ~~6~~ ~~8~~ WEEKS

The store opens in two weeks, and Dad still hasn't
spoken to Wishbone. I thought about going to the
radio station, but I'm mad at Wishbone, too. How
can you steal from your own brother? And how can
you pretend to be a stranger to your own nephew?

It's all I can think about as I do doughnuts in the parking lot with the shopping cart racer. Alex is kicking his soccer ball against the back wall of the lot. We've been out here all morning. I swing the racer a little too close to Grandma as she steps out of her greenhouse with two fern plants.

"Boy, if you get near my plants, I'm gonna plant this cane on your Black butt."

"Sorry, Grandma," I say as I lean away from her.

Grandma has replaced all the overgrown weeds that used to surround the store with flowers and plants. Inside of the store, Grandma's plants are hanging in front of all the windows. Next to Grandma's greenhouse, Mr. Reedy is unloading paint cans from his car.

"Careful now, boys," Mr. Reedy warns. "Don't knock over any of this paint."

Dad pokes his head through the kitchen door and calls for me.

"My man, come out front," he says. "I've got something to show you."

"Look up."

Dad points to three signs attached to the building above the front doors. Alex and I read the sign on top.

The words *Sunset Cookies* look like they belong on a baseball jersey. There's a gigantic swoosh underneath. Under the right side of the swoosh, there's a bigger-than-life image of Dad. He's wearing his straw hat and…a dashiki. He points to a giant cookie across from him. The giant cookie is twenty times bigger than the giant Dad above our heads. Six chocolate chips as big as mountain peaks rise out of the cookie. Five pecans the size of tree trunks are scattered between them. Dad's finger is the only thing keeping this giant cookie from rolling onto him.

I can't believe this. My dad is on Sunset Strip with all of the other giants on billboards. I look down the street at the billboard above the Rock and Roll Ralphs. Dad looks WAY cooler than those old-timey soldiers. In fact, Dad is the only Black face I see on any of these Sunset Strip billboards. He's definitely the only one wearing a dashiki.

"This is a vibe, Dad." Then I point at the giant cookie above our heads and say, "It's perfect. Just the right amount of chips. And check out those pecans poking through. THIS is a good cookie!"

Alex, Mr. Reedy, and Grandma come around the corner and stare up at Dad and the giant cookie. Mr. Reedy holds his instant camera.

"Why don't you grab a chair from inside and have a seat right here? I want to get a photo of you two under the sign."

Each of the glass doors now has the Sunset Cookies swoosh logo painted on it. Under each one it reads THE FINEST IN CHOCOLATE CHIP COOKIES SINCE 1976. Dad carries out a wooden chair and sets it down right under the giant cookie. It looks like it might fall on us at any moment.

Mr. Reedy tries to hold his camera steady, but it's no use. His Parkinson's is bad today. Alex sees him struggling and gently takes the camera from him.

"Here, Dad. Is it okay if I do it?"

Mr. Reedy hands him the camera. "Thanks, son," he says.

"Anytime, Dad. I don't mind."

Alex holds up the camera. Dad pulls me next to him and puts his arm over my shoulder. I stare up at the giant cookie. Alex snaps the photo, and the film shoots out the front of the camera. We all gather around it as the image slowly appears.

"Nice job, Alex," Mr. Reedy says. "Your first cookie portrait."

Dad looks at the photo and gives me a kiss on the cheek. " And it's our second grand opening," he says.

Back in the parking lot, Dad helps Mr. Reedy unload the last of the paint cans. Mr. Reedy rubs his hands.

"We'll need some help if we want this finished in time for the grand opening," Mr. Reedy explains. "This lot really should be painted all at once. If we had enough people we could do it in one afternoon. The paint would dry overnight. No one would have to worry about walking on wet paint, and cars could drive onto the lot the next day."

One day to paint the parking lot? I know exactly what to do.

"If I can find painters, Mr. Reedy, can you show them your sketch and tell them what to do?" I ask.

"You know painters?"

Mr. Reedy has his doubts. He looks at Dad. Dad looks at me. I look at Alex.

"Don't look at me!" Alex says. "I don't know anybody who paints."

Dad trusts me. "Go find your painters, but do not leave the block. You hear me?"

"Promise," I say. "No detours. No distractions."

I jump into the racer, and Alex pushes us off the parking lot. I know where to go first. At the corner, I tell Alex to turn left. We roll to the bus bench halfway down the block. I get out of the cart and sit.

Alex is confused. I don't blame him.

"What are you doing?" he asks.

"I'm waiting."

"For what?"

"For the bus."

Staring at the traffic, Alex and I wait on the bus bench. We wait. And wait. Suddenly...

"Duuuude..." says a familiar hippie voice.

Sure enough, here comes Cosmo carrying his surfboard. He arrives at the bus bench just as the RTD Sunset Express arrives. Cosmo gives me a high five and introduces himself to Alex. He looks at our racer with respect.

Cosmo reads the sign on the front. "The Sunset Cookie Racer. This is sweet, dude. You got your own set of wheels. That's what I need."

I follow Cosmo onto the bus. Alex stays with the racer. John Moses greets me and immediately asks if Dad knows where I am.

"Don't worry. I'm not taking the bus today. We're painting a mural on the parking lot," I say. "Can you both come and help? We only have one day to do it."

"Far out," says Cosmo. "Art expands the mind. The Surfer Society and I will be there."

"Great!" I say. "It's tomorrow."

John Moses nods his head and says, "I'll put in for a day off. I could use some time in the sun."

"Thanks, guys. See you tomorrow. Let's meet at ten before it starts getting too hot. Tell Aunt Thelma if you see her."

I step off the bus, and John pulls away. Alex stares in disbelief.

"Ellis, you're like the mayor of Sunset Strip. How do you talk to all of these people so easily?"

I get back in the racer and tell him, "I don't know. Maybe it's the dashiki. I definitely feel braver when I wear it."

Riding the Parking Lot Wave

It's painting day. Cosmo, the Surfer Society, John Moses, Alex, and I are lined up against the wall of the parking lot. Mr. Reedy stands in front of us like a coach pumping up his team before the big game.

"Painting together is a lot like making music together," he says. "It's a conversation. It's important to watch and listen to each other."

Grandma sticks her head out of her greenhouse. "That's right," she shouts across the parking lot. "Listening is tougher than talking."

"Right on!" Cosmo shouts back across the parking lot. "Grandma's got it going on."

Grandma steps out of her greenhouse. She walks over to Cosmo and points her cane at his stomach. I'm not sure she understands that Cosmo gave her a compliment.

"You watch your mouth," she warns him. "I don't need no greasy-haired white boy back talking me. Not today."

Cosmo immediately straightens up and pulls his long hair from his face. He sounds like I did talking to Mrs. Cook on my last day of school. "Yes, ma'am," he says politely. The Surfer Society tries to keep from laughing.

Grandma huffs and leaves the parking lot to tend to her plants in the store. Mr. Reedy continues explaining how to paint. He gives us big rollers— the kind that painters use to paint houses. Next, he hands everyone an open can of paint and sends us to a different corner of the parking lot. Alex and I set our cans of paint in front of Grandma's greenhouse. Cosmo and the Surfer Society take their paint cans to the back kitchen door, and John Moses stands by the driveway. A can of orange paint sits by his feet.

"Get started and have fun," Mr. Reedy says. "We've got more paint when you run out. I'm going to get some sandwiches for everyone." Mr. Reedy drives off the parking lot, leaving us to start the mural.

I get on my hands and knees, stick my roller in my red paint, and glop it on the ground. The pavement sucks it up like a sponge. This is not the same as painting on a piece of construction paper. It's going to take FOREVER to paint the ground with this roller. Across the lot, Cosmo stares at his paint roller covered in deep blue paint.

"Duuude," he says in wonder. "It's like holding a wave in my hand."

Cosmo bends over and begins making king-size sweeping motions with his roller. It *does* look like huge waves on the ground. He dips his roller back in the paint, raises it above his head, and faces the Surfer Society. Blue paint runs down his arm.

"Everyone, gather around."

Alex and I walk across the parking lot and join them. We all stand in a circle around Cosmo.

"Today, we shall chase the wave across this parking lot and ride it all the way to the cookie kingdom," Cosmo declares.

The Surfer Society dip their paint rollers and follow Cosmo as they ride his parking lot wave. Unfortunately, the paint from their rollers soaks up in the dry concrete. The blue wave quickly fades away. Across the lot, John Moses struggles to reach the ground with his orange paint roller.

"Man, my back is NOT made for this." He sighs. "Too many hours sittin' on that bus. Ellis, I may have to pass on all of this painting stuff."

There has to be a better way to paint the parking lot. Luckily, I have an idea. Well, it's really Cosmo's idea.

We just need to ride the wave.

"Hold on, everyone. I'll be right back. Alex, come with me."

We run through the kitchen and grab the last of the cardboard boxes from our clubhouse. We bring them back to the parking lot, and I rip off the sides. I hand them to Cosmo and the Surfer Society. Everyone is now circled around me as I explain.

"If we pour the cans on the ground, we can slide on the paint using this cardboard. We can ride a bigger wave...and get more paint on the ground."

Cosmo takes off his shirt and ties it around his head. Then he spills John's can of orange paint in front of him.

"I'm with you, cookie kid. Surf's up!" Cosmo belly flops onto the cardboard. He slides across the pavement, leaving a glowing orange streak behind him. A few of the Surfer Society kids follow him. The scrawny surfer walks up to Alex and me.

"Let's ride this wave together, dudes."

I pour my red paint in front of me. Alex pours his yellow paint, and the scrawny surfer slops his blue paint on the ground.

"When I say 'go,'" he tells us. "Ready. Set. GO!"

We sit down on our cardboard after running a few steps. Smears of red, yellow, and blue paint cross with Cosmo's orange streak. They look like fat paintbrush strokes in the middle of the parking lot. John Moses shakes his head.

"This don't look *anything* like that man's sketch," he says. "It looks pretty funky, though."

Funky? That's the best compliment anyone could give us. We're making a funky mural—which gives me another idea. I bet the shopping cart wheels would make a really cool pattern. I pour the last of Alex's yellow paint in a puddle next to the racer. After a short running start, I do doughnuts in the puddle. Each doughnut gets a little bigger than the last. Soon, overlapping yellow rings are crisscrossing the pavement. Now...

"Time to march! Full steam ahead!" I shout.

Another can of paint gets tossed on the ground. Cosmo, the Surfer Society, Alex, and I plop our shoes into the paint then follow each other in a single-file line all the way to the kitchen door. It looks like an invisible family is hungry for cookies.

The afternoon sun has gotten really hot, but it hasn't slowed us. Soon the ground is filled with layers of painted lines, circles, zigzags, curves, splashes, and just plain silly shapes. We all stand

in the center of our mural looking at the kaleido-scope of color surrounding us.

"I love it," I say. "It *is* funky."

"Off the hook," says the surfer kid who wants my dashiki.

The freckled, sunburned kid admires our work. "We rode the wave." He puts his arms around Alex and me. "You two dudes are alright for middle schoolers."

We all turn when we hear a horn honk. Mr. Reedy

has pulled up to the edge of the parking lot. He gets out with a bag of sandwiches. The mural stops him in his tracks. He stands on the edge of the wet paint. I can see his eyes scanning spilled paint cans, the cardboard pieces, and our paint-covered shoes—not to mention the orange paint covering Cosmo's belly. Mr. Reedy finally settles his eyes on the pattern of swishes in the center of the parking lot. I feel bad. John Moses is right. This is nothing like his sketch.

"Well…" Mr. Reedy looks for the words. "You definitely had quite a conversation here." He pauses for a moment before looking up at us. "And what a BEAUTIFUL conversation this is."

"It is?" I say. I'm not really sure.

"Yes, it is," Mr. Reedy promises. "Look at all of the wonderful designs you created. Look at the interaction between the colors."

Mr. Reedy points out shapes and patterns we didn't even know we made—like where we painted a giant heart in one section of the lot. He shows us a huge sunburst in the middle of the yellow shopping cart circles. Mr. Reedy should be an art teacher. Looking at the mural again, it looks like his abstract paintings. It also looks like a funk song. The paint on the ground rumbles and grooves like Funkadelic's "Can You Get to That." It makes my body want to move in the same way.

"I'd like to put a few finishing touches on it after the paint dries," Mr. Reedy says. "Not too much. You all painted a fabulous mural. Congratulations."

Dad sticks his head out of the kitchen door and gazes at the parking lot. We all hold our breath waiting for his reaction. Thankfully, we don't have to hold it for long. He loves it.

"Look at this," he says, admiring all of the patterns. "You all just made this neighborhood a whole lot brighter. I think we should have ourselves a block party when we open. People need to be dancing out here."

"Count us in," Cosmo says. "The Surfer Society will be here to celebrate the cookie magic." Cosmo then tells the group, "Just make sure I get permission slips from your parents."

The Cookie Is a Star

GRAND
OPENING IN
~~8~~ ~~7~~ ~~6~~ ~~5~~ ① WEEKS

It's almost impossible to remember how this place looked five weeks ago. The dirty orange carpet, the weeds, cigarette butts, trash, and peeled paint are all gone. Now it really does look like a magic cookie kingdom. Grandma's plants soak up the sun flooding the store window. The wooden floors, tables, and counter are all polished and shiny. Dad has attached a giant gold star on the door leading into the kitchen. The words *The Cookie* are painted above the star. Dad says he wants people to think the cookie is a famous celebrity and the kitchen is its dressing room. When customers walk into the store, they'll wonder what magic happens behind the door.

Three gold cookie sheets lie next to one another on top of the front counter. They aren't the plain metal ones we use for baking in the kitchen. They also aren't real gold. Dad says they're serving trays. We're going to place giant piles of freshly baked cookies on them to serve to customers. A scale with a silver bowl sits right next to the last tray. This is for weighing the cookies. Dad explains we're selling our cookies by weight. Customers can buy a quarter pound, half pound, or full pound of cookies. The last thing on the counter is a cash register.

"You, my man, are the Sunset Cookies cashier," Dad says. "I'll make the cookies in the back. You sell them in the front."

Um…I've never been a cashier before. It seems like a lot for a kid.

"Are you sure you don't want to hire an adult?" I'm not whining like I sometimes do. It just seems like Dad might be better off hiring a professional cashier. Plus, I can barely see over the counter.

"No way," Dad insists. "This is a family operation. We opened this store together and we're going to run it together—at least until you start middle school. We may need another pair of hands at some point when we can afford it. But for now, it's just the two of us." Dad pauses, then adds, "Plus Grandma and her plants."

I'm not totally convinced, but I do know Dad is right about one thing: It is our store. I want to try. First, I need to figure out how I can reach the cash register and see the customers over the counter. Meanwhile, Dad has *climbed* up on the counter just as a man in a uniform knocks on the front door. A stack of milk crates sits beside him. Dad looks over his shoulder, careful not to fall off the counter.

"Milk delivery is here," he says. "Open the door and let him in, my man."

A crisp-looking milkman enters the store wheeling a stack of milk crates on his dolly. He sets them behind the counter by the new refrigerator. This isn't a normal refrigerator. This one has a glass door and four shelves. The milkman holds out a piece of paper on a clipboard for Dad to sign, but he's busy hanging something above the counter.

"My man down there can sign for it," Dad tells the milkman.

The milkman hands me a pen and holds out his clipboard. This is my first time signing for anything. I sign my full name on the form so it's super official.

"Ellis Bailey Johnson?" he confirms, reading my signature.

"That's right," I say.

The milkman takes the pen and asks, "Your title?"

I'm not sure what that means. "Title?"

"Your job title," the milkman clarifies. "I need it for the form."

"Oh, I get it," I say. "Harmonica player and cashier."

The milkman raises his eyebrows at me, but he writes it down anyway. Then he signs his own name on the form and rips off a page from his clipboard.

Dad climbs down from the counter and gives the milkman his familiar brown bag.

"Here are some cookies for your drive," he says. "I'm guessing you don't need any milk."

The milkman pops a cookie in his mouth and smiles. He gives Dad a handshake. It looks like a secret one. There is a bump and a few slaps.

"A Black man selling cookies!" the milkman says proudly. "That's exactly what we need. More of us brothers taking ownership. Showing we can do it *all*. Mark my words, brother, one day we're gonna have a Black man in the White House." The milkman looks at me and adds, "It might be this little brother."

The milkman pops another cookie in his mouth and wheels his empty dolly toward the front of the store. I hold the door open for him. He looks down at the plastic fist on the end of my pick. He salutes me with his own fist and smiles. I close the door behind him and turn around to see the framed photo Dad hung above the counter. It's the picture of the two of us in front of the store. It looks perfect.

"Alright, my man," Dad says. "Let's get all of this milk into the refrigerator. I'll be in the back."

I examine the stack of milk crates. Each one is filled with half-pint containers of regular and chocolate milk—the kind they serve at the school cafeteria.

I lift the top crate off the stack. It's heavy. I use it to prop open the glass refrigerator door. Then I begin carefully arranging the tiny milk cartons on the shelves. I want them to look organized. I don't think customers would want to buy milk if all of the cartons were just thrown on the shelves

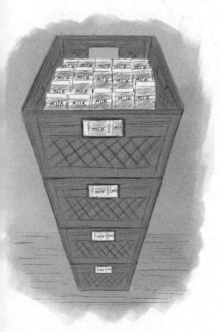

in any old way. I still remember what my kindergarten teacher, Ms. Biederman, used to say—it's all about the details, details, details.

The milk cartons look perfect. All of them face the same direction. All of them are arranged evenly. I left the top row of the refrigerator empty. I can't reach that one. Now it's time to make myself taller. I stack two of the crates upside down, slide them over to the counter, and stand on them. I look at the cash register. Something amazing has happened.

"Hey, Dad!" I shout to the kitchen. "Come here."

Dad meets me at the cash register.

"Well, look at you. My young man is starting to sprout."

I grew! I don't need to stand on two crates. I jump off and remove one from the stack. Then I get back up again. Yep, I only need one milk crate to reach the cash register...barely. It doesn't matter, though. I grew. Milk crates don't lie.

Dad walks through the kitchen door and stands in front of the cash register. He pretends he's a customer.

"One pound of chocolate chip cookies, please."

"Yes, sir. Coming right up."

I scoop an imaginary bunch of cookies onto the scale. Then I pour them into an imaginary bag and hand it to Dad.

"That'll be three dollars, sir."

Dad reaches into his pocket and hands me a ten-dollar bill. I punch the numbers on the cash register keys. The drawer opens.

"Hey, Dad," I say. "There's no money in here. How do I give you change?"

"Dang, that's right." Dad snaps his fingers. "We'll have to get some petty cash before we open. I'll make sure I remember." He reaches into his imaginary bag and takes a bite of an invisible cookie. "Great cookie," he says. "I'll be back." Then he reminds me, "Always look people in the eye. Always say thank you."

I jump off the milk crate and follow Dad back into the kitchen just as the sound of Sunset Boulevard traffic fills the store. Someone has opened the front door and walked in. Oops, I forgot to lock it after the milkman left. I hear a voice that reminds me of the one a month ago when Alex and I were pulling out the carpet.

"What's going on in here?" the voice asks.

Oh no. Did that drunk man come back to bully us?

Hershel the Handyman

My heart is beating in my throat again. I'm afraid to turn around. I hear Dad answer the question the same way he did last time.

"We're opening up a store selling chocolate chip cookies."

The voice responds, "Of course you are. I've tasted them. They're great."

Wait a minute. I know that voice. It's not the drunk bully. It's the man who fixed our shopping cart. My heart drops back into my chest as I turn around.

"Hey, cookie kid," the man calls out. "I figured this must be your place. How's the shopping cart?"

"It's great!" I tell him. "I turned it into a racer."

I realize I should introduce him to my dad. Ugh. I don't know his name. I really need to do a better job at remembering people's names in my neighborhood. I try anyway.

"Dad, this is my friend who fixed our shopping cart."

Lucky for me, I don't need to remember his name. He waves from the front of the store and introduces himself.

"Hershel," the man says. "Hershel Sykes. Do you mind if I bring my shopping cart inside? I don't want anyone stealing it."

Dad does not want Hershel's shopping cart on his brand-new wooden floors. He suggests that he bring it around to the parking lot.

Back at the lot, Hershel parks his shopping cart next to mine. He spots the sign on the front of my racer.

"The Sunset Cookie Racer," he reads. "That's smart. I should name my cart." He holds out his hand. "Hershel Sykes at your service."

"Ellis Johnson." I shake Hershel's dirty hand. I'll wash it later. I don't want to be rude. Hershel looks at the freshly painted mural under his feet.

"Did you do this?" he asks.

"With my friends." I show Hershel the pattern I made with the shopping cart wheels.

"I can tell that a lot of love went into this," Hershel says.

Now that his shopping cart is safe in the parking lot, Dad invites Hershel inside for some cookies. His eyes light up seeing all of the equipment in the kitchen. He knows the names of everything. He points to the mixer.

"The Commodore Diamond Elite!" Hershel says. "That's the granddaddy of all mixers. You got yourself a good one there." He rubs his finger against the sealed crack on the bowl. "Yeah, these bowls crack easily. It's the one drawback of the Diamond. You need to be careful with this type of glue you used. The moisture from the cookie dough will mess it up after a while."

Hershel looks at the knobs on the mixer. He adjusts one of them.

"Your speed is too fast for cookie dough," he says. "If you mix it too fast the batter will get stiff."

"That's exactly what happened with my last batch," Dad says. "I couldn't figure it out." Dad pats Hershel on the back to thank him. Then he asks him the question I was thinking. "Hershel, how do you know about all of this baking equipment?"

Hershel explains that he used to work at a big bakery. They made bread for grocery stores. He was a floor manager, which means he had to order all of the supplies and make sure the equipment didn't break. It sounds like it was a lot of responsibility. It also sounds like he liked his job a lot, because Hershel is talking about it the same way I talk about my harmonica. He excuses himself and leaves the kitchen. Through the open kitchen door, Dad and I see him digging into his shopping cart. He pulls out some type of framed photo and carries it back into the kitchen. Hershel hands it to Dad. It's an award.

CHAMPION BAKERY

EMPLOYEE OF THE MONTH

HERSHEL SYKES

SIGNATURE

"I got this right before the bakery went out of business," Hershel tells us. "Things can change so fast. You just never know."

How can someone run an entire bakery one minute and be *homeless* the next? It just seems impossible. Hershel is so smart. He knows how to fix shopping carts. He knows all sorts of details about baking. He already taught us something about mixing cookie dough.

"Hershel, do you want to work here?"

"Uh…excuse me?" Dad asks.

I remind Dad, "*You* were the one who said we needed an extra pair of hands."

"Yes, *later*, when the store is actually open and you go back to school."

Hershel interrupts us and accepts my job offer. "I would be honored to work for you two fine men."

Hershel extends his dirty hand to Dad. I can see Dad thinking. He's scratching his beard. He wrinkles his forehead. His eyes squeeze shut. He pinches the bridge of his nose. Finally, his eyes open, and Dad grabs Hershel's hand.

"Welcome to Sunset Cookies, Hershel," Dad says with a smile. "Listen, brother, we're gonna need to do something about..."

Hershel interrupts Dad before he can finish. "Don't worry, sir. I just got a room at the shelter on Gower and Santa Monica. I'll get a hot shower and some clean clothes." Hershel picks up his Employee of the Month award from the table. He looks us in the eye and says, "Thank you. I'll make you proud. You'll see."

Dad tells Hershel to come to work tomorrow morning. We walk him to the parking lot, say goodbye, and watch him push his shopping cart away. I look down at the mural. I still see new shapes and patterns every time I stare at it. Some of these patterns wouldn't even *exist* if Hershel hadn't fixed our shopping cart. All of the chocolate chips could have melted in the shopping cart if Hershel wasn't there to fix our wheel. He's going to be a great employee. I know it.

"Everyone deserves a second chance, Dad."

Dad nods his head and scratches his beard. "That's right, my man. They do." We follow the painted footsteps back to the kitchen door as I hear Dad say to himself, "Maybe he'll work on commission. How am I going to pay for help? I'm not even paying myself yet."

Sunset Cookies opens in less than a week. Summer vacation is almost over. If I can get Dad to hire Hershel, I *have* to be able to get him and his brother back together. Dad says this is a family business. Our entire family should be here for the grand opening.

Boom, Boom, Out
Go the Lights

In only a few days, Hershel has really helped the store. He resealed the mixing bowl crack and fixed the broken shelves in the greenhouse from the Sunset Racer incident. He told Dad where he can buy big bags of chocolate chips so he doesn't have to wait on Rock and Roll Ralphs all the time. He also keeps his hands super clean now.

"Hershel's the best person I've ever hired for a job," I tell Alex. We're listening to the A-side of our newest album, *Maggot Brain* by Funkadelic. It's the one with "Can You Get to That."

"Hershel is the *only* person you've ever hired for a job," Alex corrects me. He drops the needle on the third song.

"Exactly!" I agree. "And look what a great job he's doing. He even organized our clubhouse for us. He's the best person I've ever hired."

"It's hard to argue with that," Alex agrees. He starts bobbing his head to "Can You Get to That." The groove has got him.

"*See*? Now you know what I was talking about," I tell Alex. "That's the funk." Alex's entire body is moving like a slow-motion jumping bean. "Don't fight the funk," I warn him. "It's too strong."

I play along with my harmonica, closing the clubhouse door so we don't disturb Dad in the kitchen. I stop for a second when I see myself. My Afro is flat on one side. I pull out my pick and fix it. I'm so happy that Hershel hung this mirror on the back of the door. It helps to see how I look when I'm playing harmonica—and make sure my Afro stays round.

Alex is now completely overwhelmed by the funk. He's dancing on a short pile of brown sugar sacks.

"Be careful!" I warn. "Remember the sugar disaster. We open the store tomorrow. Dad and I can't afford any setbacks."

Alex ignores me. "Chill out, Ellis," he says. "I'm fine. It's the funk. I can't control it." He jumps off the brown sugar sacks and lands next to me. Then he speaks in a way that sounds more serious than I've ever heard Alex speak. "How are we gonna get Wishbone here for the grand opening? Any person who knows about this music can't be all bad," he says. "Wishbone deserves a second chance, Ellis. And... we need more funk. We've gotta figure this out."

Alex is right. I've been thinking the same thing. Wishbone understands stuff that other people don't. He must have had his reasons for what he did at the Rat Trap. Plus, people change. I'm a *totally* different person than I was at ten. I just can't understand why...

...the power just went out.

The funk has stopped cold, and the clubhouse is dark. Dad and Hershel immediately open the door to make sure we're okay. Then Dad asks me a simple but scary question.

"Ellis, you mailed the electric bill, right?"

Did I? I'm trying to remember. I've got to think about this quickly before it becomes obvious I'm not answering.

"Ellis, what happened?" Dad asks. I guess I took too long to answer. Okay, now I need to change the subject while I think about this some more. Maybe I can ask him if the equipment is okay. WAIT! I remember. I DID mail it. No. Wait. I *didn't* mail it. I left it with Wishbone at the mothership. Not good. I'm changing the subject.

"Dad, is the equipment okay?"

Dad's not going for it. I can barely see him in the dark, but I can tell his forehead is wrinkled. I need to tell him the truth.

"Dad, I left it at the radio station. But Wishbone promised he would mail it."

Dad kicks the door. I don't think I've ever seen

him kick *anything* before. I try to explain. Of course Wishbone mailed the electric bill. Why *wouldn't* he mail it? Dad's in no mood for listening. He's already left the clubhouse. He makes his way to the front of the store, talking to himself like that man in the back of the bus.

"Melvin messed me up at the Rat Trap," Dad grumbles. "That fool is *not* gonna mess me up again."

Dad storms down Sunset Boulevard toward KIRA. This is not the way I wanted to get them back together again. Alex and Hershel follow me out the store. We all watch Dad walk away. I'm nervous. Should I go with him? I hope he stays safe. I yell down the street.

"Dad! You come right back. No detours. No distractions."

Grandma walks around the corner from the side of the store. She's holding some trash in her hand. It must have blown down the street into her plants.

"That looks like Junior down there," she says.

"It *is*, Grandma," I tell her. "He's going to see Wishbone...I mean Uncle Melvin."

"Well, it's about time," Grandma says. "Two grown men working on the same block after all these years and still not speaking to each other. Them boys are fools."

Hershel offers to take the trash from Grandma. "Let me throw this away for you, Mrs. Johnson. The power went out inside. I hope it comes on soon, or else all of our milk and cookie dough are going to go bad."

Grandma is not happy to hear about the power going out again.

THWACK!

"There ain't *no* way my Junior is losing his cookie dough and milk the day before his grand opening," Grandma yells onto the street.

Hershel leans over and whispers to me, "Don't take this the wrong way, Ellis, but your grandma reminds me of some of the people at the shelter. Is she okay?"

I tell Hershel this is normal for Grandma. He'll

get used to it. Meanwhile, Grandma keeps huffing and puffing outside of the store. Then she finally says it.

"NOT TODAY, SATAN!"

Alex and I run to the front door and press our faces against the glass. It's still dark inside. Hershel tries to make sense of what's happening. He must think we're characters. In fact, I am *positive* we look like characters out here on Sunset.

"Them lights come on, boy?" Grandma asks.

"No, Grandma," I say, looking through the glass.

Grandma can't believe it. "You kidding me."

As Grandma decides whether or not she wants to yell again on the corner, Hershel points to a blue repair truck across the street. It's parking next to a wooden utility pole standing in between two palm trees. The words DEPARTMENT OF WATER AND POWER are on the side of the truck. A man with a hard hat gets out and begins to climb the tall post.

"It's about time," Hershel says. "The power is always going off on this block. Some of these places lose it once a day."

Wishbone *did* mail the electric bill! I yell across

Sunset to the repairman, asking if he is fixing the power for the store. A harness is wrapped around the pole and connected to his waist. He looks like a mountain climber.

"The whole block," the repairman shouts back from the top of the utility pole. "The transformer is unstable. It should have been replaced a long time ago. Someone just reported it today."

"That's right," Grandma says, pointing up at the sky. "I reported it to the man upstairs."

Grandma did it again! Like I said, I don't ask questions. More importantly, though, Dad's about to blame Wishbone for something he didn't do. Grandma must be thinking the same thing.

"Go on down there before your daddy makes a fool of himself."

Before I know it, Alex is standing with the Sunset Cookie Racer. "Hop in," he says. "My legs are longer. I'll get you there fast."

As Alex races me toward KIRA, I hear Hershel shouting from behind us. "Keep an eye on your shopping cart! Don't let anyone steal it."

Reunion on the Mothership

Alex stops our racer in front of the KIRA Radio stairs. I jump out just as Dad walks inside the station. I ask Alex if he's coming with me.

"Nah," he answers. "I'm gonna wait here and keep an eye on the shopping cart. Good luck, Ellis."

We give each other our secret handshake, and I run up the stairs. I open the door and run smack into Dad standing at the front desk. He's talking to the woman in braids. He doesn't even seem to notice we're all in the dark.

"Please, tell me where to find Melvin Johnson?"

The woman in braids is confused. "Melvin Johnson? There's no Melvin Johnson here, sir."

Then she spots me. "Hey, honey, you're Wishbone's friend," she says sweetly. "How come you're always coming around when the lights are out?"

I correct her. "Actually, I'm Wishbone's nephew." Then I point to Dad and tell her, "This is his brother."

"Well, ain't that something. Wishbone has family. I would have never guessed that. Wishbone is…different."

"Believe me, I know," Dad says.

The woman in braids hands me a flashlight and says, "You know the way, honey."

I show Dad down the hallway. I shine the light on the floor so he can see the Milky Way carpet, but he doesn't care about our indoor spacewalk. We arrive at the mothership. I try to explain to Dad about the repair truck. I want him to know that the power went out EVERYWHERE. We *are* standing in the dark, after all. Dad won't hear it. He pulls the door open and steps into the mothership.

"Melvin, where is my electric bill?" Dad calls out in the darkness. "I am NOT letting you mess this up. It's taken me eight years to get past the Rat Trap. You are NOT getting in my way again."

Dad grabs the flashlight from my hand. He shines it around the darkened mothership, looking for Wishbone. I'm pretty sure I know where I can find him. For a brief moment, the flashlight shines on Wishbone's Musical Constellation of Blackness on the ceiling. I catch a glimpse of the posters before Dad moves the beam of light to the back of the mothership. Dad shifts the flashlight again when he hears Wishbone's voice.

"Fool, I ain't getting in NOBODY'S way," he says. "I did my crime, paid my time, and the future is *mine*. I put your electric bill in the mail, fool. I ain't messin' with your cookie store."

Suddenly, the lights flicker back on. Dad searches around for Wishbone. I point to the L-shaped desk. Dad looks down. He sees Wishbone and his giant Afro squeezed underneath. They stare at each other like two boxers before a fight. It's like all of the air has been sucked out of the room. It feels very funky right now on the mothership.

Then, out of nowhere, Dad starts laughing. I mean laughing *hard*. He's laughing harder than I laughed when Alex missed the basket in the Rock and Roll Ralphs. He sits down on the floor in front of Wishbone.

"Man, you're *still* scared of the dark?" Dad asks once he gets his laughter under control.

Wishbone squeezes out from under his desk. "It ain't no thing," he says. The tremble in his voice says it *is* a thing. Wishbone is *definitely* still scared of the dark.

I sit down cross-legged next to Dad and Wishbone. All three of us face one another on the floor. Our knees are touching.

Dad tells a story about Wishbone sleeping on Aunt Della's sofa bed with the lights on. "At least Aunt Della's sofa bed didn't have springs popping out of it," I say while nudging Dad.

"What's up with that, Pops?" Wishbone scolds

Dad. "You can't get Big Brother a decent sofa bed? My man deserves better." Wishbone looks at me and says, "Your pops was always tight with the cash."

Dad shoots Wishbone the same look he gives me when I cross the line. If I were Wishbone, I wouldn't say *anything* to Dad about money. I look at the two of them. They're talking. They're laughing. This is the moment I dreamed about. I have so many questions to ask them, but I don't want to interrupt. I want them to keep talking to each other forever.

A knock on the door does interrupt them, though. A jumpy man enters. He has sideburns shaped like pork chops.

"Wishbone!" the man squeals. He sounds like he sucked in a bunch of helium. "Are you forgetting something? If you want to keep your job, you better get your mouth on that microphone." The squealing man with the sideburns shuts the door.

"Oh, snap." Wishbone jumps up into his seat. He pulls the microphone close and pushes the red button. Once again, his voice turns to velvet. He speaks to his radio audience while placing an album on his turntable.

"Brothers and sisters, Wishbone owes you his deepest apologies," he says. "But we've got the power runnin' and more funk comin'. This here is the Godfather of Funk, Soul Brother Number One, Mr. Dynamite. The one and only…"

"James Brown!" Dad and Wishbone say the name together.

The needle drops and Wishbone rises. A deep funk groove explodes through the speakers. Dad and Wishbone instantly start dancing. They face each other, shaking invisible Hula-Hoops around their butts. They give each other a fist bump before shouting in each other's face, *"Get down with your bad self."* I look at the label on the spinning record.

JAMES BROWN
"Say It Loud, I'm Black and I'm Proud"
King Records

"Opening night at the Rat Trap," Dad says to Wishbone. "James Brown takes the stage."

Wishbone points to me and says, "Big Brother bouncing in his stroller. I'll never forget it. You had the funk from *day one*!"

Wow! I saw James Brown at the Rat Trap when I was baby? Now I need to figure out who *is* James Brown. Dad starts flipping through the record collection. Every now and then, he pulls out an album and stares at it.

"You've got some solid music here, little brother," Dad compliments Wishbone. "I might have to start listening to your show."

Dad and Wishbone remind me of Alex and me in the clubhouse. *Alex!* He's still outside, probably wondering what to do.

"Um, Dad, I think we should get going. There are still things to do for the grand opening tomorrow."

It's no use. He's lost in the funk.

"You go on without me, my man, I trust you," Dad says, shaking his imaginary Hula-Hoop. "I'm gonna watch Melvin do his thing for a little bit." Dad watches Wishbone cue the next album. He looks proud of him. "Little Melvin on the radio," he says.

"Quiet," Wishbone begs Dad. "Melvin is dead and gone. This here is Wishbone. Keeping it real…"

"ALWAYS!" the three of us shout.

I turn, leaving Dad and Wishbone lost in the funk. Before I open the door to the mothership, I remove Wishbone's photo from my pocket. Now is my chance to put it back on the wall without him knowing. I carefully slide it behind the postcards and other objects. I almost have the photo returned when I hear Wishbone.

"Go on, Big Brother. Keep it. And don't be stealing no more stuff. That mess will get you in trouble. Ain't that right, Pops?"

I turn around. Dad and Wishbone are looking right at me. They look exactly like brothers. How come I never saw it before?

"Family is tougher than time, my man," Dad says. "And we don't take things that don't belong to us. Now get on back to the store. We've got a grand opening tomorrow."

The Grand Opening

This is it. My first chance to come out on top. The grand opening is one minute away. All eyes are on me.

"Are you ready, Ellis?" Dad asks.

I slowly step onto my milk crate. Dad stands next to me, piling freshly baked cookies onto the gold trays. Grandma is watering her last plant. Showtime.

"Ten, nine, eight..." Dad moves to the front of the store.

"Seven, six, five..." I straighten my pick and check my dashiki.

"Four, three, two…" Dad unlocks the front door. *"ONE!"*

Nothing. No one is here. Dad steps outside the door. He looks both ways down Sunset Boulevard. Nobody. We wait a few minutes. We wait a few minutes longer. I stay on the milk crate just in case. After nearly an hour, I step off and ask, "Dad, what's happening? How come no one is here?" I thought I did a pretty good job getting customers. Where are my friends from the bus? Where's Jordan?

Dad's forehead is getting wrinkled. He takes a cookie from the gold tray. He looks at it like a long-lost friend before taking a bite. "That's a good cookie," he says looking around the store. "And this idea is a hit. I know it."

"I'm sorry, Dad. I should have taken out the racer a few more times to find more customers."

"*Sorry?* Ellis, this store is already a success. It brought our family together. And these are good cookies."

Dad chews and swallows as our first customer arrives. It's Wishbone.

"July twenty-six, nineteen *seventy*-six," he announces to the empty room. "This is a day for the record books, brothers and sisters. Sunset Cookies has come alive!"

Dad and I tell Wishbone it's not exactly alive. He's the only one here.

"Pops, Big Brother, you worry too much. Chill," Wishbone says. "You built it, and they WILL come. Now allow me to be your customer NUMBER one."

Wishbone steps to the counter and orders. I pour his cookies into a brown paper bag and hand it to him. "One pound, three dollars," I say. "I put a few extra in there for you." The cash register drawer opens. It's empty. Oh boy. Dad forgot the petty cash.

"Man, I *knew* I was gonna forget something today," Dad says, annoyed with himself.

Wishbone reaches under his long dashiki and sticks his hand in his pant pocket. He pulls out a thick wad of money. It's rolled up as big as his fist with a fat rubber band around it. He hands it to me.

"Take this for your petty cash. And a tip," he says before turning to Dad. "I owe you some cash anyway, Pops. Consider it a down payment."

Dad takes the money before I can touch it. He asks Wishbone where he got it. Wishbone is a little irritated at the question.

"Where did I get this cash? Hey, we don't need to talk about that. It's all cool, Pops. It ain't *no* thing. I promise."

Dad wants to believe him. Dad *has* to believe him. Wishbone's his brother. He unrolls the bills and asks me to arrange them in the cash register drawer. Then he gives Wishbone their secret handshake. Wishbone looks at his watch.

"Oh, snap," he says. "The countdown has begun, get ready for cookie lovers on the *run*." Wishbone begins counting...

"Ten, nine, eight..." Dad looks at me.

"Seven, six, five..." I look at Dad.

"Four, three, two..." Grandma looks at Wishbone.

"Melvin, don't make me get a switch on you," Grandma warns.

"ONE!"

Wishbone walks to the front of the store and opens the door. There is a line of people. Wishbone lets them inside. He hollers across the store to Dad, "You should listen to my radio show, Pops. I've been talking about your store for *weeks*—ever since Big Brother here brought me some cookies."

Dad hugs and thanks his brother. "Now I gotta bake more cookies," he says. Dad squeezes my shoulder and tells me, "You hold it down, my man." He returns to the kitchen. Wishbone and Grandma follow him back, shutting The Cookie's dressing room door behind them. It's just me in the front— alone with a store full of cookie lovers. I scoop cookies, serve milk, collect cash, and make change. Things are moving really fast. It's hard to keep up. I say "thank you" to every customer, but sometimes I forget to look them in the eye like Dad asked me.

I give a woman two dollars' change for her cookies without looking up.

"You're a good cashier," the lady says. "Maybe you want to sell groceries instead of cookies."

I raise my head. It's the cashier from the Rock and Roll Ralphs. "Thanks," I say. "But cookies are the family business. I'm going to stay here."

The cashier walks out of the store just as an

RTD city bus pulls up front. I catch a glimpse of the sign. It reads SUNSET COOKIES EXPRESS. The door opens and John Moses walks off. He helps Aunt Thelma down the steps. She's holding a bag of oranges. They stand in the back of the line. John Moses calls up to me.

"You're looking good up there, buddy. Take your time."

"I got you some good oranges," Aunt Thelma says.

Hershel brings out a fresh tray of cookies. He's looking a little stressed. "Ellis, your dad needs you in the kitchen. He said come right away. I'll watch the front."

Back in the kitchen, I've never seen Dad so busy. He pulls some hot cookies from the oven. Then he moves to the mixing bowl full of batter. I ask him what he needs when Grandma steps inside and shrieks.

"MY POCKETBOOK! Someone stole my pocketbook," Grandma shouts. "I NEVER take my pocketbook off my arm."

"Calm down, Mama. I'm sure you just set it down somewhere. Just think."

Grandma shoots back at Dad, "I didn't set it down nowhere. And I'll tell you what I think." Grandma points her cane at me. "I think your friend Alex stole it. I always thought that white boy looked a little shady. You see him wearing that hooded sweatshirt and them baggy shorts? An' I don't like that shifty handshake he gives you."

"Mama, Alex is Ellis's best friend. Stop that nonsense. I don't have time for this right now," Dad says. "You see those customers out there? We got cookies to sell. Did you check in your greenhouse?"

Grandma snatches my arm. "Boy, come here. You gonna help me find my pocketbook."

I need to work in the front. That's my job. Why is Grandma giving me the "boy, come here" routine and dragging me out back? And why is she talking that way about Alex? She pulls me through the door and onto the parking lot. Alex is standing in front of us with Grandma's pocketbook on his arm. This has to be a mistake. Alex would never... What the...

Sunset Cookies Summer
Block Party

SURPRISE!"

Alex is surrounded by *everyone* in the neighborhood. The parking lot is packed with people. I see Wishbone, Mr. and Mrs. Reedy, Courtney, Cosmo and the Surfer Society, John Moses, Aunt Thelma, the Bubblegum Moms, and the woman in braids. Some of my friends from school are here, too. There's Brad Katz. Even Amanda Freeman came, wearing a bright flowery Hawaiian dress.

Alex hands Grandma her pocketbook and gives

her the secret handshake. What is happening? The universe has turned upside down. Alex laughs at my blank stare.

"Sometimes you gotta take a chance, right, Ellis?" he says. "HA! We got you!"

Grandma joins in. "Boy, you should have seen the look on your face when I said your sweet friend stole my pocketbook."

I've been pranked by own family. I can't believe this. I also have to admit, it was a GOOD prank. I give Alex a high five.

"You're the best friend ever, Alex," I tell him. It's true. He really is.

"You too," he says. "I think your family is great."

Dad comes out of the kitchen holding a baking sheet. There's a giant cookie on it. A message is written in chocolate chips.

"Dad, today's July twenty-sixth. My birthday's in August. Did you forget?"

"Nope," Dad says. "We're celebrating a week early. Today is YOUR day. See all of these people? They're here because of *you*, my man. They know about this cookie store because of YOU. You fine-tuned our recipe, you helped get our ingredients, you fixed this store, and you got us our customers, Ellis Bailey Johnson."

Dad starts singing "Happy Birthday." Everyone in the parking lot joins him. It feels like all of Hollywood is singing to me. They clap and cheer. I blow out the single candle stuck in between the words "Birthday" and "Ellis." This is the best day of my life.

The only thing missing is Mom. I can't wait until she sees the store. I bet when she does, she'll forgive Dad. Maybe they'll even get back together. Who knows? Look what happened with Dad and Wishbone. Everyone deserves a second chance.

Speaking of Wishbone, I spot him in the corner of the parking lot in front of Grandma's greenhouse.

He's set up two turntables and a microphone. He taps on the mic then switches on his velvety voice.

"Brothers and sisters," he announces. "The sun is up and it's time to get *down*. We got cookies in the oven and serious funk a-comin'. I want everyone on the dance floor. We gonna boogie with the birthday boy."

Wishbone drops the needle, and the parking lot is instantly transformed into an outdoor dance club. EVERYONE has the funk. Grandma's purse swings around her arm as she dances with Alex.

"You play it, Melvin!" she yells.

Wishbone puts his hand over the microphone and gets Grandma's attention. "It's Wishbone, Mama. Don't be calling me Melvin. That was me before I *found* me. Melvin is dead and gone." He takes his hand off the microphone and shouts to the crowd, "Keeping it real, baby. Keeping it real ALWAYS!"

The funk is getting deeper. Cosmo and Aunt Thelma are bumping their butts. Mr. and Mrs. Reedy dance like they are in an old black-and-white movie. People from all around the neighborhood pour into the parking lot. Dad hands out cookies to everyone from one of his gold trays. Hershel has filled the Sunset Cookie Racer with milk cartons. He pushes it through the crowd.

"Today, the cookies are on us!" Dad shouts above the music. "You all tell your friends and bring them back with you." Dad looks around at the crowded cookie block party. I hear him say more to himself than the crowd, "I might do this every year. If I can afford it."

Across the parking lot, Brad Katz is standing with his father. I really need to thank him for the conversion factor from that math quiz. "Hey, Brad," I say. "Thanks for coming to my party. Also, I wanna say thanks for all of the help in math last year."

Brad's dad looks at him. "You helped this boy with his math?"

"Ellis sat behind me in class. We were...study partners." Brad leans over and whispers, "You and your dad sure made a lot of cookies. Aren't conversion factors the coolest?"

Did he really say conversion factors are the coolest? While funk music is blaring across a multicolored parking lot? And free chocolate chip cookies are being handed out? It's all I can do to resist laughing. Luckily, I'm distracted by a tap on my shoulder.

"Jordan, you made it."

"I wouldn't mi-mi-miss it. Neither would my dad. He's over th-th-th-there."

I see Jordan's father following my dad across the parking lot chattering nonstop. Poor Dad.

"I b-b-brought you a gift for your g-g-g-grand opening."

Jordan hands me an envelope. I open it and read the top of the paper inside.

"'Gift certificate.'"

"It's for T-T-Tiny…"

"Tiny Naylor's!" I interrupt. "Sorry. I was just excited. Thanks, Jordan. This is super nice of you."

"M-m-maybe we can all have a di-di-divorced kids d-dinner to-to-together."

"That'd be great."

Jordan spots his father hovering around my dad. "Anyway, I'm going to g-g-get sss-some more coo-cookies. And get my dad to st-st-stop talking."

"Okay. I'll find you later and introduce you to Alex."

Jordan brushes by a girl as he beelines across the parking lot. A *beautiful* girl. She has an Afro like mine. Brightly beaded bracelets hang around her wrists. Her bell-bottom jeans are covered in patches. Before I can catch my breath, she walks over to me. She's even prettier up close. She holds out her hand and looks me square in the eye.

"Hi, I'm Jada. I like your dashiki, and your cookies are amazing. My mom heard about your store listening to KIRA. She drove us all the way here from Baldwin Hills."

Jada lets go of my hand. I wish she didn't. "Well, good luck with the store. Happy birthday. Maybe I'll see you again."

Before I can say anything, Jada disappears into the crowd. Alex steps up next to me, holding Grandma's purse.

"Your grandma asked me to hold it," Alex explains. I see her dancing with John Moses. Aunt Thelma doesn't look happy about it. "Who was that girl?"

I wish I knew. And I hope I find out. Alex and I put our arms around each other. We stand on our painted footsteps looking at the dancing crowd. I gotta admit it. This has been the best summer of my life.

"I think middle school is going to be amazing, Alex. I just have a feeling. Things are changing."

"Yeah, I think so. Make sure you bring some cookies on the first day."

"Oh, for sure. These cookies are going to make us famous at middle school. We're going to be V.I.P.s"

"V.I.P.?" Alex asks.

"Very important person."

We give each other our secret handshake—one palm slap, two fist bumps, then grab pinky fingers.

One Last Customer

The sun is setting on Sunset Boulevard. The cookie store is closed for the day. I'm stacking milk cartons in the refrigerator. And thinking of Jada. Grandma, Dad, and Wishbone sit at one of the tables in front. Grandma's pantyhose are down around her ankles while her swollen feet rest on a chair. Wishbone is shuffling a deck of playing cards.

"Alright, now, the name of the game is Tonk," Wishbone says as he gives cards to Grandma and Dad. "First one to get rid of their cards wins."

Grandma, Dad, and Wishbone study their cards

when a knock at the front door interrupts them. I stand up on the milk crate to see who's here. It's a man in a gray three-piece suit. A large bus is parked behind him. It's not like the RTD city bus. This one is fancy and looks more like a camper. All of the windows are dark. The man has a thin mustache— almost like it was drawn with a black marker and sprinkled with salt. In fact, he looks like an older version of...

MUDDY WATERS! Muddy Waters is standing outside of our cookie store! He looks just like the album cover—only older. Wishbone and Dad leap up and open the door. Muddy Waters steps in. He stares at Wishbone and Dad.

"Will you look at this? The brothers Johnson," he says. "How long has it been? Last time I saw you two, we was tearing it up at the Rat Trap. Man, we had 'em going that night, didn't we?"

"Yes, sir, Mr. Waters." Wishbone sounds like me talking to Grandma. He's *very* polite. "We sure enjoyed having you play our club."

"You playin' Tonk?" he says, eyeing the cards on the table. "Me and the boys on the tour bus got a game goin' on right now. We're headin' up to San Francisco for a show and got ourselves a sweet tooth. Some woman at that Rock and Roll Ralphs said they got some good cookies here."

"The finest chocolate chip cookies since 1976," I say.

Muddy Waters looks over at me at the counter and smiles. "Boy, you look like the spittin' image of my first harmonica player, Little Walter. Whose boy is this?"

Dad puts his arm around me. "This is my young man, Ellis. He was in diapers when you played at the Rat Trap."

"You don't say?" Muddy puts his hands on my shoulders. MUDDY WATERS IS PUTTING HIS HANDS ON MY SHOULDERS! "You grew up real good, Ellis Johnson."

"Thank you, Mr. Waters." I muster all of my courage to look him in the eye and tell him, "You're my favorite singer of all time."

"And your daddy and uncle ran my favorite music club of all time. Hated to see it go. But now you all selling cookies." Muddy Waters points to the gold star on the kitchen door and asks Dad, "Got any more in that dressing room?"

That's my cue. I rush into the kitchen, quickly fill three brown paper bags of cookies, and bring them to the table. I offer them to Muddy Waters. Dad reaches over to tuck my harmonica back in my pocket.

"Careful, my man. You're about to lose this."

"Well, look at you!" Muddy Waters says. "You *are* Little Walter. Go ahead an' blow that harp for me, son."

"C'mon, Big Brother," Wishbone urges me. "Show Muddy Waters what you can do with that thing."

I take a moment to push my heart out of my throat. Then I pull my harmonica out of my pocket and place it to my lips. I blow four notes that I know Muddy Waters will recognize.

Duh DUH duh DUHN

Muddy Waters sings right on cue.

Now, when I was a young boy
Duh DUH duh DUHN
At the age of five
Duh DUH duh DUHN

Dad and Wishbone join him on the next two lines.

My mother said I was gonna be
Duh DUH duh DUHN
The greatest man alive
Duh DUH duh DUHN
I'm a man
Duh DUH duh DUHN
I spell M-

Muddy Waters pulls me to him and gives me a hug. "Now, that's a man, alright. You got it there. Keep playing that blues. I'm gonna call you Howlin' Johnson."

Muddy Waters just gave me a blues name. I've got my own blues name! Finally. I guess that's how you get a blues name. This is how you reinvent yourself.

You just keep looking for clues until they all add up to something. Muddy pulls a cookie from one of the bags and takes a seat between Grandma and Dad.

"Woo! THAT'S a good cookie!" Muddy reaches over and places his hands on Grandma's bad knees. She looks like she might faint. "Ms. Johnson, you must be proud of these boys," he says. "Fine Black men, all three of them."

Muddy Waters looks around the table at all of us. "A Black family selling cookies on the Sunset Strip. This here is a beautiful family. A *perfect* family." Muddy Waters pops another cookie in his mouth, points to the deck of cards, and says to Wishbone, "Deal me in, brother. San Francisco can wait."

"Straight away, Mr. Waters," Wishbone says. "I hope you can make those cards sing."

Muddy Waters studies his cards closely. Without looking away, he says to me, "Pull up a chair, son. Blow me some more of that harmonica while I play these cards."

I grab a chair and squeeze in between Muddy Waters and my dad. I look around the table. It's just another Friday night having cookies and milk on the Sunset Strip. This is my family. We create magic from nothing. We know that sometimes you gotta take a chance. My family starts businesses and makes music. My family welcomes *everyone*. We know who we are. We listen even when it's tough. My family has made mistakes, but we stick together because family is tougher than time.

This has been Ellis Howlin' Johnson from Hollywood, California. Home of Sunset Cookies. The finest in chocolate chip cookies since 1976.

Keeping it real. ALWAYS!

A NOTE FROM THE AUTHOR

Dear Reader,

I want to thank you for giving me your time so I could share my story. Reading a book is a big commitment and there are lots of books to read. I'm glad you chose mine—or maybe it was chosen for you. Either way, I'm glad you're here.

I also want to let you in on a little secret. Many of the moments in this book happened to me as they did to Ellis. Way back in the 1970s, I was an insecure kid from a badly broken home. Now I'm a divorced dad. There's a little bit of me in Ellis and a little bit of me in Dad in the pages you just read. I still remember being called the N-word in the front of my father's cookie store like it was yesterday. The shock is long gone, but some of the sadness of that racism still remains. That's the thing about getting older: Some sadness disappears, and some sticks around. Some of it repeats itself. But getting older isn't a total downer. Like all of life, it's beautiful, full of twists, turns, and seriously cool surprises. Writing this book is one of those surprises. If someone had told me at age eleven that my childhood would be interesting enough to write a book, there's no way I would have believed it.

Also like Ellis in this book, I was a Black kid growing up in a largely white area where I was embraced by an extended family of friends. I am still grateful these people *saw* me—even if there was no one else around who *looked* like me. This protective circle helped me forget my troubles as a child and face my childhood troubles as an adult. I hope you have people like this in your life. I hope they manage to stick around forever. I'd like to thank some of them now in writing. You might recognize a few of these names (or versions of them). Other names won't mean anything to you, but they are important to me, so thanks for reading anyway.

To my California childhood circle: Alex Reid,

Courtney Reid, Jennifer Brill, Brandi Umbach. Thank you for unknowingly softening the blows of some hard early-life hits.

To the Reid family, Katz family, Mazursky family, Harris family, Elliott family, Brossy family, Roderick and Jackie Sykes, and BJ Markel. More than anyone, you have tended to my childhood scars and helped me outlast them. Thank you.

To my ex-wife, Marta, thank you for long ago believing I could be a father when I was unsure myself.

And then there are the ones who gave me space to revisit my childhood as a writer...

My endless gratitude to my editor, Lisa Yoskowitz, for believing in this first-time author. Your patient guidance and artful insight were a wonder to witness and a blessing to receive. Thanks to Andy Ball, Karina Granda, Emilie Polster, Victoria Stapleton, Sydney Tillman, and everyone at Little, Brown for welcoming me so warmly into your family of authors.

Thank you, Jesse Murphy, David Kuhn, Penny Moore, Arlie Johnson, Elan Fingles, Hope Bryant, Jason Karlov, Amanda Taber, and Bryan Thompson for watching my back and finding a home for this story.

A huge thanks to my youngest child, Harper, for months of reading these chapters aloud after dinner. You gave these characters their first voice and delivered some of the sweetest memories of my life.

Thank you to my oldest kiddo, Piper, for exploring this side of your family tree with me. Our journeys back together have helped break some chains and close some loops.

And once again, to my son, Ellis, thanks for creating the initial spark that set this book in motion. I hope it helps you to understand yourself, me, and us a bit more.

Thanks also to Sarah Amos, Courtney Silk, Jinny Cho, Robert Burke Warren, Michael Dutton, Robert Dowling, and Karen Tangorra for cheering me on, keeping me fed, and believing in my ability to pull this off. I have felt your love.

Lastly, I want to thank all of the great Delta and Chicago bluesmen of the 1940s, '50s, and '60s. Their lives and music have taught me the trials, tribulations, and triumphs of being Black in America. They are my heroes who helped me reinvent myself as the Black man I wish to be.

That's it, dear reader. Thanks again for witnessing Ellis's story and letting me tell you a bit about my own. Good luck on your own journey. Whatever your age, color, size, hair, family, or neighborhood, I hope you always celebrate and share what is unique about you. The world needs you to shine bright.

Stay safe and keep the faith,

Shawn Amos

THE FINEST IN
CHOCOLATE
CHIP
COOKIES
SINCE 1976

CHOCOLATE CHIP COOKIE RECIPE

Ingredients

> 2 medium eggs
>
> 2 sticks salted butter
>
> 1 teaspoon baking soda
>
> 1/2 teaspoon salt
>
> 3/4 cup granulated sugar
>
> 3/4 cup packed brown sugar
>
> 1 teaspoon vanilla extract
>
> 2 1/4 cups all-purpose flour
>
> 1 cup pecans
>
> 1 cup semisweet chocolate chips
>
> 1 pinch shredded coconut

Directions

1. Put eggs, butter, baking soda, salt, sugars, and vanilla extract into the bowl of a stand mixer. Mix at low speed for 1 minute, then on high for 4 minutes.

2. With the mixer off, add flour, then blend at medium speed for 2 1/2 minutes.

3. Break pecans by hand. Fold into batter with the mixer set to low.

4. Add chocolate chips and coconut last, with mixer set to low speed.

5. Refrigerate batter overnight in an 8-inch-square container.

6. The next day, cut batter into 8-inch by 2-inch rectangles. Sprinkle with flour (you don't want your hands sticky). Then, using two hands, roll on countertop until each rectangle looks like a snake that's 1 inch in diameter.

7. Preheat oven to 350 degrees F (electric) or 375 degrees F (gas). Use a nonstick cookie sheet. Pinch off 1-inch bits from the roll of cookie dough and place on the

sheet in even rows. Make each cookie unique.

8. Bake for 12 minutes. Your cookies should be as brown on top as they are on the bottom. They should also be crispy.

Make them with an adult, and eat them with a cold glass of milk, your favorite songs, family, and friends.

DJ WISHBONE'S PLAYLIST

Blues, funk, and grooves for the whole family. Don't fight it!

"Mannish Boy"

Muddy Waters

From the album *The Real Folk Blues*

(Chess Records)

"Can You Get to That"

Funkadelic

From the album *Maggot Brain*

(Westbound Records)

"Get It Together"

The Jackson 5

From the album *Get It Together*

(Motown Records)

"Spoonful"

Howlin' Wolf

From the single "Spoonful"

(Chess Records)

"Hoodoo Man Blues"

Junior Wells

From the album *Hoodoo Man Blues*

(Delmark Records)

"(We've Got To) Come Together"

The Reverend Shawn Amos

From the album *The Reverend Shawn Amos Breaks It Down*

(Put Together Music)

"Say It Loud—I'm Black and I'm Proud"

James Brown

From the album *Say It Loud—I'm Black and I'm Proud*

(King Records)

"Hollywood Swinging"

Kool & the Gang

From the album *Wild and Peaceful*

(De-Lite Records)

"(Are You Ready) Do the Bus Stop"

The Fatback Band

From the album *Raising Hell*

(Polydor Records)

"Family Affair"

Sly & the Family Stone

From the album *There's a Riot Goin' On*

(Epic Records)

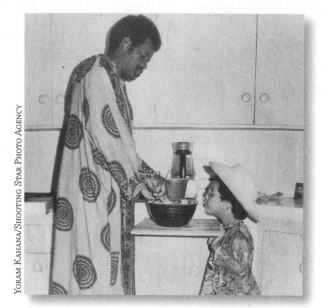

Shawn watches his dad mix cookie dough in his ceramic bowl (Hollywood, 1975).

SHAWN ELLIS AMOS

grew up in Hollywood, California, with divorced parents. In 1975, he helped his dad, Wally "Famous" Amos, open the world's first chocolate chip cookie store on the corner of Sunset Boulevard and Formosa Avenue. Shawn is now a divorced dad to his only son, Ellis, and his two daughters, Piper and Harper. He sings and plays harmonica as blues singer "The Reverend Shawn Amos." *Cookies and Milk* is his first novel.